MURDER

BOOK TWO: SKYWOLF

www.CreativeTexts.com

Creative Texts Publishers products are available at special discounts for bulk purchase for sale promotions, premiums, fund-raising, and educational needs. For details, write Creative Texts Publishers, PO Box 50, Barto, PA 19504, or visit www.creativetexts.com

Murder on the Trinity: Book Two: Skywolf
by Sue Land

A COLD WEST BOOK

Published by Creative Texts Publishers
PO Box 50
Barto, PA 19504
www.creativetexts.com

ISBN: 9781653257423

MURDER ON THE TRINITY
BOOK TWO: SKYWOLF

CREATIVE TEXTS PUBLISHERS

Barto, PA

TABLE OF CONTENTS

CHAPTER 1

Joseph Skywolf stood on the small front porch of his cedar cabin, enjoying the sound of an early morning waking up. Taking a deep breath, he inhaled the sweet aroma of the spring shower that had just slipped away, mingled with the strong smell of the East Texas pines. It felt good to be alive, and he was looking forward to seeing Lillian this morning; he had something important to ask her. Joseph, if he was honest, would admit that he was a little worried about Lillian's answer. Uncle Tall was a great Medicine Man and had assured him that Lillian would say yes to his proposal. Joseph, however, was not sure just how much Uncle Tall knew about women and their hearts.

Despite the peacefulness of the morning, there was a restlessness that kept edging its way into Joseph's brain. Something was not right, and whatever it was, he knew it would make an impact on him. Whatever that impact would be, it would not be good.

Born on the Comanche Indian reservation in Lawton,

Oklahoma, Joseph had learned not only to walk in the white man's world but to walk in the footsteps of his ancestors. He was of two worlds growing up. There were a lot of hard lessons he learned from being a "Redskin." Hoping to make a difference in both of his worlds, Joseph had gone on to teach Native American History at Oklahoma University. Early one morning, as he stood on top of the clock tower on the university grounds, he contemplated the possibilities of flying off the roof. He would become an eagle, fly away from the Whiteman's school and all the crap that came with it. Growing up, his Uncle Tall had told him many stories of how his people could change life forms. So, he would become an eagle and fly away. It was, perhaps, a good thing that the tower clock chose to strike the seven A.M. call to morning classes about that time. It snapped him out of the trance he seemed to have fallen into. By noon that same day, Joseph had resigned his teaching position, packed up his belongings, and headed for Texas to visit the one man he called a friend, Sheriff Jonathan Lawrence.

It wasn't only Jonathan who he was coming to see, but he was returning to the East Texas, Piney Woods, which had long had a hold on him. As a child and teenage boy, he had spent days, weeks, and months trudging through the forest, an area that covered over six hundred thousand acres. He was soon able to throw off the shackles of the collegiate world, and he found that rescuing city sleeker's who wandered off into the forest, only to become lost, took up most of his time. The rest of his time he filled by being Jonathan's deputy.

The sudden sound of the bray of a jackass broke into Joseph's reminiscing as it announced a phone call. Glancing at the number, a smile lit up his face, and he cheerfully answered, "Good morning, Lillian. You're up bright and early."

Lillian Marcus, the dispatcher for the Liberty County Sheriff's office, and the woman who kept a sparkle in his eyes returned his greeting.

"Good morning, Joseph," she responded. Then her voice changed to one of seriousness, as she demanded, "What have you been up to since our sheriff's departure, on his honeymoon yesterday?"

"Not a damn thing," he answered, and asked, "Why, what's up?"

"Got a call from Austin this morning. A Texas Ranger by the name of Lucas Wilson is looking to talk with you," she told him, and added, "He will be here at noon."

"Well, as far as I can recall, I haven't done anything to cross the path of a Texas Mountie," he said, "but I'm on my way. I'll bring you a donut or two. You can stand a little fattening up," he told her, with a light chuckle. And before Lillian could call him any number of choice words in her vocabulary, he disconnected.

Pitching the remains of his coffee over the porch rail, Joseph took one last lung-full of the sweet, clean country air. Liberty was not a big city, but it was big enough to have some of the same problems as a big city, such as excessive gas emissions and heavy traffic. The natural Parks, starting in early spring to the last of fall, drew thousands of tourists. If the camping, hunting, fishing, and trekking didn't cast a net for tourists, the Alabama-Coushatta Indian Reservation did, with their casinos. The town had grown with the opening of new businesses, such as fast-food drive-ins and economy motels, which offered a place to lay the head of a weary traveler. All that growth was just the incentive that pushed Joseph further and further back into the forest.

As he entered the sheriff's office, Joseph felt a restless itch move back up his spine. "Yep, something definitely was not right."

Lillian was sitting at her desk talking with a young man dressed in a white Stetson hat, a long-sleeved starched white shirt, and tight-fitting blue jeans. Even before Joseph saw the gun on the young man's hip, and the badge on his chest, he knew this had to be the Texas Ranger. Lucas Wilson stood about five-feet-eleven-inches tall, weighed around a hundred seventy-five pounds, had dark brown hair that reached to his shoulders and flipped up at the ends, brown eyes, and a small brown mustache. The whole picture was that of a Cowboy, from the run-down heels on his cowboy boots, to his tight-fitting blue jeans.

Looking at the young Ranger, and then at Joseph, Lillian made the introductions, which Joseph acknowledged with an inquiry, "I'd say you coming to see me from Austin makes this business, not pleasure."

Lucas nodded, "Yes sir, if you have a few minutes?" The thick Australian accent was evident, and once again Joseph felt the crawling sensation up his nerve ends that warned him of coming trouble.

Pointing to the closed door across from Lillian's desk, Joseph told him, "We can talk in the Sheriff's office." After entering the office, Joseph motioned for Lucas to sit down in the chair opposite the sheriff's desk. Joseph sat down behind Jonathan's desk.

"You've come a pretty distance. So, tell me, what can I do for you?" Joseph knew he was not going to like the answer to his question.

"Three days ago, Thomas McCain gave the authorities the slip, and we believe he was, or is, headed for Liberty." Lucas leaned forward and continued. "McCain is believed to be a hired assassin, and his target is here."

Joseph was becoming more agitated, waiting for the other shoe to drop, "We were able to track McCain to the Reservation," Lucas explained.

And so, the other shoe had dropped; Joseph's. "You need someone to go into the Res and bring him out?"

"Yes sir," Lucas answered, with a small smile of apology. "You've come highly recommended. You know the reservation and the forest better than anyone."

"Yeah," Joseph said, obviously not impressed, adding, "And I just happen to be a Redskin."

Lucas shifted uncomfortably in his chair and said, "Yes sir, I guess that is another reason. McCain is half Cherokee and he was raised in these piney woods."

Joseph took a deep breath and released it slowly, as he asked, "You brought the file, I assume?"

"I left a picture of McCain and a full description, but there is no file," Lucas told him.

Joseph shook his head, sighing, and placed his arms on the desk in front of him and leaned forward, his manner no longer welcoming. "If a man wants my help, he needs to start out trying not to throw a pile of manure on me. Now suppose we start again, and this time you tell me the truth."

Lucas was quiet for several moments, then, slowly, a smile tugged at the corner of his mouth as he said, "I was told you were too smart for me to pull off this ruse. My name is Lucas Wilson. My accent tells you I'm not native-born. Figured you'd know there was no way I'd be a Texas Ranger." He paused for a moment, giving Joseph time to insert, "Yeah, now tell me something I don't know."

"I am state law, the Governor's police. The part about McCain is true. I do need your help tracking him. I know he is not going to stay hidden. He will come out again. He has a mission."

Joseph interrupted him, and asked, "You know his mission?"

"We think we do. The Feds have been watching McCain for a while; they just didn't have enough to pull him in. McCain was once a legal advisor for several international investment firms. He was in Houston when he received a tip that warned him he was about to be picked up by the FBI. That's when he skipped."

Sitting back in his chair, Joseph's frown deepened, as he asked, "You're the Governor's man, and you're chasing a fed fugitive?"

Lucas nodded and said, "The Governor's niece . . . she and McCain had a thing. The Governor thinks she might have been the one who gave the warning."

"And your job is what? To shut the guy up before he can cast a cloud over your boss?" Joseph questioned, with a great deal of sarcasm.

A spark of anger lit Lucas' eyes, but faded quickly, as he answered, "I need to catch the guy before he carries out his assignment. The niece has enough to face with the tipoff, but, she could also be charged with helping him carry out his hit."

Joseph sat for a few moments silently digesting what Lucas has just told him. Finally, he asked, "Where did you lose McCain?"

"The Rangers tracked him to the pit stop at the roadside park, right below the I45 Bridge, over the Trinity River," Lucas said, adding, "The Rangers figured he broke his neck when he jumped. They brought in dogs and tracked north of the bridge, as well as South. The dogs hit his scent and followed it until the Res. The Rangers stopped, reported in, and were told to pull back."

"Am I to assume you do not plan on telling me who McCain's target is?" Joseph asked.

Lucas shook his head and said, regretfully, "Not unless I have to. Which I hope I don't."

Joseph studied Lucas for a thoughtful moment and did not like that old feeling crawling up his spine. "And what would the factor be that would cause you to let me in on this secret target?"

Now deadly serious, Lucas told him, "To save the target's life."

Joseph stood and walked around the desk.

"Meet me at the Res police headquarters in an hour. You're going in with me. Bring in one of those tracking dogs. If McCain is part Indian, he just might be hard to track"

A big grin lit up Lucas' face, as he jumped to his feet, saying, "I was hoping you'd say that. What about supplies?"

This time it was Joseph's time to flash a grin.

"Don't worry about that. I'll bring what we need."

Lucas hesitated for a moment before saying, "The Governor would like for it not be known that I work for him. The naysayers would love to start mouthing that he is trying a cover-up."

"Yeah." Joseph didn't like Lucas' reasoning, but he would accept it for now.

Leaving the office, Joseph led Lucas over to Lillian's desk.

"Lillian, you need to get an APB out on this McCain. And get a hold of George Seville, out at the Res, and tell him that Ranger Wilson and I will be packing in this evening. If he would like to join us on this manhunt, I'd be happy to have him."

Lillian's smile did not reach her eyes, but before she could make any response, Joseph leaned across her desk and planted a swift kiss on her startled lips.

"I'll keep in touch, don't worry," he whispers.

Before she could make any sort of a reply, he walked out, with Lucas on his heels. Outside, Joseph turned and warned Lucas, "One word and I'll leave you in the deepest, remotest part of those woods, and you'll have to find your own way out."

Holding his right hand up, palm forward, Lucas tried his best not to laugh. "No sir, not a word, but I got to admit, I've never seen that method used before to keep your staff happy."

Lucas opened his truck door, got in and instructed Lucas, "Get the dog and meet me at the Res headquarters. I'm assuming you ride, just in case we go in by horseback."

Lucas nodded, and, speaking with a deepened accent, said, "Yes sir, I got a buckle in 2015 from the NPRA for bronc riding. Will that do?"

As he shut the truck door, Joseph replied, "It'll have to do, won't it?" He threw the truck into reverse and applied the gas, squealing the tires as he sped off.

Lucas gave out a soft whistle as he watched Joseph drive away. Joseph Skywolf was proving to be everything Lucas had been told he would be.

Exactly one hour later, Joseph pulled up in front of the reservation police structure. Once out of his truck, he reached back inside and retrieved two backpacks. He handed one to Lucas, who had walked up to stand beside him. Glancing around and not seeing any sign of the dog, Joseph turned back to Lucas and asked, "Where's your tracking dog?"

Putting two fingers to his lips, Lucas gave a shrill whistle, and what seemed like a split second later, a black and white German shepherd came bounding out of a nearby wooded grove, and stopped at Lucas' feet.

Slapping the dog affectionately on the rump, Lucas praised it. "Good girl, Sam, good girl." Looking at Joseph, he made the introductions. "Deputy, this is Fraulein Samantha Land, better known as Sam, the best dang tracker anywhere."

Studying Samantha for a few moments, Joseph stepped forward and held out the back of his hand for the dog to sniff. He spoke softly, saying, "It's good to meet you, Sam." Samantha sniffed the back of Joseph's hand and slowly licked it, as if to say, "OK, we can be friends." Only thing was, Lucas would swear that Sam and Joseph thoroughly understood each other, and knew exactly what each other thought.

Smiling at Lucas, Joseph said, "Be interesting to see how the Sheriff's new bride reacts to the pooch sharing her name."

Hearing his name, Joseph turned to greet George Seville. "Appreciate you coming out on this, George."

"No problem. My men and I looked at your entry point yesterday. . . figured we could save you some time," Seville told Joseph before he turned to Lucas to say, "I reckon you're the Ranger that's gonna tag along."

Holding his hand out, Lucas was impressed with Seville's appearance. . . "Dang if the guy didn't look every bit the Old West Redskin!" He had long, black hair flowing past the shoulders, black eyes, roughly five-foot-ten, a strong chiseled chin and a hawk nose. Seville was dressed in a blue cotton shirt, jeans, and leather boots. Two eagle feathers were tied in his hair.

Breaking from his thoughts, Lucas acknowledged Seville's greeting, "Yeah, that's me. Thanks for letting me tag along."

Before any more chit-chat could continue, Seville's phone chirped. Slipping the cell phone off his belt, Seville snapped, "This better be important!"

A male voice on the other end responded in excited tones. "It is, Boss. This is Lindy. Our fugitive hit one of the camps before daylight. One dead, one wounded. He's on the run again, and this time he's armed. A Rugger and lots of shells."

Seville was stunned for a moment. He took a deep breath and told Lindy, "I'm on my way. I'll call for an ambulance. How bad is he wounded?"

"Not bad. He'll live. We've got the camp roped off," Lindy told him.

"Alright." Seville took one more deep breath, and released it, saying, "Sit tight. I'll be there ASAP."

Hitting the disconnect button, Seville turned to answer the question on both Joseph's and Lucas' face, telling them, "Your guy just killed one of our campers and wounded another. He is also now armed with a Rugger."

"Damn!" Joseph's curse did little to release his flare of anger. "Where is this camp?" he asked.

"Camp entrance is right off State 190. It's the Camp Tombigbee. We can go by four-wheeler and cut across from here."

Lucas and Joseph grabbed their backpacks from their vehicles and followed George to his four-wheel, off-road vehicle. As they back up, Joseph removed his cell phone from his belt and punched the courthouse number. When Lillian answered, he instructed her to dispatch a CSI tech out to the campsite. Before hanging up, he told her, "I'll be back tonight."

Lillian hurriedly asked the question that had been bothering her. "What made you decide to help in tracking McCain?"

"The guy didn't escape to run off into the woods and live like Rambo," he told her, and added, "He has an agenda, and that would include a way to get out of the country. He has a helper, and we need to find out who that is."

"Okay, but if our guy is that sharp, you need to watch your back," Lillian warned.

Without replying, Joseph disconnected, and as he looked over his shoulder, he asked Lucas, "Where's the dog?"

"She won't lose us."

Grinning, Joseph said, "I was more concerned we might lose her." Silent for a moment, Joseph finally asked, "Who tipped off McCain? Don't give me the Governor's niece crap."

Lucas gave a lopsided smile, as he answered, "Wondering how long it would take you to ask that. It was one of the women who work in the Governor's office. Seems she and McCain had a thing going on."

"Where's the woman now?" Joseph asked, waiting to see if Lucas was going to be upfront with him.

"Well, considerable thought was given to having her arrested, but again, the Governor wanted…."

Joseph interrupted and finished Lucas' sentence. "Doesn't want any bad press. So, where is she?"

"An attorney was appointed for her, and a deal was made that she would remain under house arrest at the Capital, incognito, until McCain is apprehended."

Joseph held off asking further questions. They could

wait until they arrived at the campsite. Half an hour later they drove in to find the deputies waiting. As the deputies walked up, one of them, Lindy, Joseph assumed, greeted them.

"We kept all the curious on-lookers back, out of the way. A couple packed up and was gonna leave, but we stopped them. Figured you might want to talk to them."

George nodded and told Joseph, "I'll take the nervous Nellies while you and Ranger Wilson check out the scene. Lindy will go with you and answer any questions you might have.

"Appreciate it," Joseph told George. He then turned to Lucas as sirens announced the approaching CSI team. "Put Sam on a perimeter sweep and see if she can pick up anything," he told Lucas."

Nodding, Lucas opened his backpack, took out a plastic bag with a t-shirt in it, removed the shirt, and whistled for Sam. As she came running up, Lucas held the shirt down for her to sniff. He spoke softly, saying, "Find, Sam, find."

Joseph watched as the dog went immediately from a happy-go-lucky, excited pet, to a sharp, alert and obedient dog. Sniffing around the front entrance of the small pine cabin, Sam took only a few seconds to sound the alert bark, and she was off to track, with Lucas close behind her.

With the arrival of the crime lab and the ambulance for the wounded man inside the cabin, Joseph waited to enter the cabin with the medical examiner and the emergency techs.

Once inside the cabin, Joseph took his time, moving slowly about the room. He stopped at the small nightstand and turned to ask the Medical Examiner, Robert Dean, "Does the victim have a cell phone on him?"

Looking up, Dean shook his head, and said, "Naw, why?"

Joseph picked up a small, white cord that had an electrical plug on one end, and a small, single-prong plug on the other before he answered. "Because the charge cord is here, but no phone. I'd say our perp has the missing cell phone."

Dean stood up and motioned for the two men who were waiting with the gurney to remove the body. He walked over to Joseph as he pulled off the rubber gloves he wore to examine the deceased. Placing them in a plastic zip-lock bag, he took a deep breath and proceeded to give his initial report.

"Our deceased's cause of death is a pretty open and shut case. He was shot twice in the chest."

"Thanks. If anything unexpected comes up, let me know."

Dean gave a sharp wave and walked out of the cabin, picking up his trash as he went. Joseph took one last look around and went back outside just in time to see the EMS Techs put the wounded victim in the ambulance. Seville saw him and walked over, but before either man could speak, Joseph's phone sounded.

Joseph's answer was crisp, "Skywolf."

"Our guy has taken a turn East and is headed back to the Interstate," Lucas told him.

"He has a cell phone, and he's called for a ride. Come on back. It'll be dark in a couple of hours. Come on back. You and I are going back to the Sheriff's office. We need to talk," Joseph informed Lucas, in a not-too-kindly tone.

"Sam and I can catch him before he makes the interstate, "Lucas told him.

"Yeah, and you and Sam can get a bullet in your brain

just as easy. Can't say I mind too much about you, but I would hate to see Sam get shot." Joseph replied. Not waiting for a counter-reply, he disconnected and joined Seville, who was waiting by the four-wheel vehicle.

After Joseph was seated, Seville backed out and headed back toward the reservation headquarters, but not before he asked, "Wilson really a Texas Ranger?"

"Well. . ." Lucas started to lie, but stopped, figuring, "What the hell," and then unloaded, "Naw, he's law, but no Ranger. Can you have a couple of your guys follow my fugitive on out? Let me know if he takes a turn?"

Seville agreed to help, saying, "Sure, but you owe me."

Grinning, Joseph nodded. "Agreed. Next time one of yours' pulls a drunken brawl in town, I'll escort him home; no charges."

"Sounds good to me," Seville said, but not willing to let go of the subject of Lucas, he asked, "So what's Wilson's connection with your perp?"

"He's trying to find him before any more damage is done," Joseph said, and added, "Damage to who, and what is my question?"

"Seems to me you got a cougar by the tail," Seville

said.

    "Yeah," Joseph nodded in agreement.

CHAPTER *2*

The drive back to town was done in silence. Both men were deep in their thoughts, and each knew there was reckoning waiting back at the sheriff's office. Joseph knew he had been fed only half the story on McCain, and he also knew before one more step was taken in apprehending the fugitive, he was going to get the full story.

Back in the sheriff's office, Joseph started things off by letting Lucas know he was tired of being played a fool.

"McCain has a friend, or a safe hole, here in town. That's who he called to pick him up. Who is it?" His tone let Lucas know he wanted and expected information, and that there was to be no more evading the facts.

Lucas wasn't sure the deputy was going to buy what he had to say but he could see no reason to avoid telling what he did know.

"I've got no idea who McCain has here. Had no idea he had anyone." Seeing the doubt on Joseph's face, Lucas repeated, "Honestly, I do not know."

Before Joseph could reply, his intercom sounded. He pushed the button and answered, "Yes, Lillian."

"We've got a lock on our dead camper's cell," Lillian told him.

"Where?" asked Joseph.

"It's out at the old McQuoid mill," she said.

The words were barely out of Lillian's mouth before Joseph and Lucas ran past her, with Sam on their heels, out to the car. With sirens blasting, and with burning rubber, they sped out of the parking lot. The drive took less than twenty minutes. Stopping a quarter of a mile down the red dirt road that led from the old mill, Joseph, Lucas, and Sam got out and checked their guns. Joseph wasn't worried about Lucas, nor his ability to handle himself in a gun battle, he just hoped the young bronc rider was a good shot.

"I want McCain alive, if possible," he told Lucas, and added, "Have Sam stay here."

Lucas nodded, and quietly put Sam in the stay command, and asked, "What about his buddy?"

Ignoring the crooked grin on Lucas' face, Joseph said, "If possible. Yeah." With those last words, the two started moving toward the old mill, keeping to the cover of the woods and surrounding brush.

They stopped about ten yards back from the mill and surveyed the perimeter. There was no vehicle parked in front, and it looked deserted. The two men moved quietly toward the old mill. A few yards from the entrance, Joseph motioned for Lucas to stay put, and he moved quietly up to the front entrance. Stooping down Joseph, moved slowly up to the window and cautiously raised his head until he could see inside the mill. Dropping back down, he motioned for Lucas to move up. Once Lucas was beside him, Joseph instructs, "I'm going in the front with a loud crash. You break the window to distract him. I don't think it will be needed 'cause our guy is laying on the floor. Kind of dark in there. Can't tell if he's lying down, taking a nap, or if he's dead."

Minutes later, Joseph's question as to whether or not the guy was alive was answered. He was very much dead; a nice little bullet hole between his eyes gave testimony to that. Joseph called for the coroner and preceded to look around the interior while Lucas went outside to start a perimeter check around the mill. Both men came up with nothing except the dead man's wallet, which contained his identification.

Kicking at a small rock, Lucas let off a little of his frustration. "Damn! We are no closer to McCain than we were."

Joseph wished he had some encouraging words for Lucas, but one thing was for sure; McCain was not leaving any loose ends. The target was still in the guy's crosshairs and he was not giving up. McCain was a professional, and there was no way, besides a bullet in his head, was he giving up.

By the time Joseph and Lucas got back to the sheriff's office, Lillian had gone home for the day. The drive back had given Joseph time to think and to rehash what Lucas had told him, as well as the many possible things he had not divulged. The bronc riding provided Lucas a good cover, but it still did not make sense that he was an agent who was acting for the Governor of Texas, chasing a federal fugitive. Hell, he was tired of being played.

The thought was digging around in his brain, searching for an answer. Pointing to the coffee, he told Lucas, "Pour yourself a cup of fresh coffee, and let's talk."

Lucas poured the cup of coffee and sat down and

watched Sam as she walked over and laid down at Joseph's feet, her eyes slowly closing in sleep. "You and Sam seemed to have bonded."

Ruffing the thick fur around the dog's neck, Joseph nodded. "Yeah, might have to talk to you about Sam having a new home."

"Yeah, we might need to do that," Lucas said, adding, "Might have to use her as a bargaining chip."

Straightening, Joseph turned his full attention to Lucas and the problem at hand.

"I want the details. What knowledge does your witness have, and who is it on? Most important who is the target?" Joseph's tone lacked any warmth, and his manner clearly showed that he was tired of being led around like a show bull with a ring in his nose.

"Six years ago, my witness worked for a charitable foundation; one of the biggest in the country. By accident, she accessed a file on one of the officer's computers. What she saw scared her, but she had enough sense to make a USB copy. She shut the computer down and made a run for it. Only thing is, when the guy turned his computer back on, it asked him if he would like to return to the same page he was last on."

"And that tells the guy someone had been nosing around," Joseph interrupted.

"Yeah, and since our witness was the last one that signed out, it was easy enough to figure out who was last in his computer files."

Taking a sip of the fast-cooling coffee, Lucas continued. "Our witness was no dummy. She skipped town that night. The next morning, she contacted a lawyer who she trusted, had him contact the Feds, and set up a meeting. She met with them and gave them the USB file she had copied. She told them she was leaving, and to let her know when or if they needed her to contact her lawyer friend. She said she would be checking back in with him every few days."

"Let me tell you the rest of the story," Joseph said, with a rising anger in his gut. "There was a leak. . . her attorney was killed, and your witness skipped for good."

Taking a deep breath, Lucas nodded and told Joseph, "The firm was deep into money laundering, and the list of those involved went up the political ladder. Our witness needed to be put into protective custody. Finding her was the problem."

"How did your witness end up here in Liberty, Texas?" Joseph asked.

Lucas hesitated for a moment before he told Joseph, "It seemed that there was one person she knew she could trust with her very life. He lived here. She asked him what she should do, and he told her to come. She was set up with a new identity and a new life, and waited for the Feds to let her friend know when she would be needed to testify. That was six years ago."

Joseph's face is emotionless, as he digested what Lucas had just told him. The seemingly constant sign of a knot growing and burning in his stomach returned with a vengeance. He reached over and picked up the desk phone, dialed, and waited for an answer on the other end. When it did, his voice was ice, as he said, "Chester, its Joseph. I need for you to take another deputy and the two of you set up a perimeter watch on Lillian's house. No one goes in or out until I get there, understood?"

"Yes sir," Chester quickly responded, but asked, hesitantly, "Is Lillian okay?"

"She's fine, Chester, just want her to stay that way,"

Joseph told him, and hung up before Chester could ask further questions.

Lucas was the first to break the drawn-out silence, by asking, "How did you know it was Lillian Marcus?"

Taking a deep breath, Joseph released it slowly, and said, "I didn't, I guessed."

Lucas shook his head and acknowledged Joseph's ability to jump to conclusions with little or no facts, just with a small amount of information. "I'd say you have a damn good guessing sense."

"Yeah," Joseph agreed, adding, "right now I am not crazy about what I see is coming."

"We'll catch McCain before he has a chance to pull anything," Lucas said, trying to assure him of something he had little faith in. Standing, he added, "Right now I need to get checked into the local motel, and you need to go talk to Ms. Marcus."

"Before we do that, I want to know your story," Joseph told Lucas, and let him know that he was tired of being played. "There is no way in hell you are just the Governor's mop-up boy. How and why are you involved?"

Lucas remained silent for several moments. He was

smart enough to know Joseph was not going to be put off.

"I had a beautiful twenty-one-year-old sister, Katie. She graduated from the University of Texas three years ago, and she got a job as a page in the State Capital. That's where she met Senator Abbott, and she went to work for him as an Aide. We never got to celebrate her twenty-second birthday with her. She went to Mexico with him and never came back, and with my last breath, I will make Abbott pay."

"So, you started working for the Governor to bring Abbott down," Joseph said, adding, "By any means?

Lucas did not hesitate with his answer. "I have been close to blowing his head off more than once. The only thing that stops me is I want the whole pie, not just a slice."

Joseph remained quiet, letting Lucas' words sink in while watching Sam, who has been curled up at his feet. Sam stood up and stretched, walked over to the sofa and jumped up on it, curled up and went back to sleep. Joseph stood and asked Lucas, "Why don't you stay here tonight? Sofa folds out and the clean sheets are inside it. Jail shower offers all the comforts of any motel. You can finish your story in the morning, like why is the Senator responsible for your sister's death."

Turning around to check out the sofa, Lucas nodded. "Sounds like a good idea to me." Smiling at Sam, he added, "Besides, I think Sam has already settled in."

Despite the knot in his gut, Joseph's smile was warm as he looked at the dog. "Shows how smart she really is," he said.

Walking out to the parking lot together, Lucas was the first to break the silence. "On the way in, I started another GPS search on our dead guy's cell phone. If I hear anything, I'll give you a call."

Frowning, Joseph asked him, "How'd you get the cell number?"

"The dead guy's buddy regained consciousness on the way in; gave the name and cell number to the EMI Tech," Lucas answered.

Opening his car door, Joseph told Lucas, "Get some rest. Tomorrow is going to be a hard one."

With that final bit of advice, Joseph drove away, his thoughts already on how he would tell Lillian someone was going to try to kill her.

Parking in front of Lillian's house, Joseph saw Chester

in his squad car parked a half a block down, so he walks over to him. Chester got out of his vehicle and greeted him. "Evening, Joseph. No one's been around. Things have been real quiet."

"Thank you, Chester. I'll take over till morning," Joseph said, but added, "I want you back before dawn, and until you are told otherwise, you don't let Lillian out of your sight."

"Sure thing, Joseph," Chester assured him, but questioned, "What's going on?"

"I'll explain everything tomorrow," Joseph told him, and turned and walked back to the house.

Joseph entered Lillian's house, trying to be as quiet as possible, so as not to wake her. In the bedroom, he undressed and slipped into the bed. Easing over to place his arm around Lillian's waist, he snuggles closer, which brought a soft, purring sound from Lillian. Joseph whispered in her ear, "Shhhh, go back to sleep. We will talk in the morning." After another soft purring sound, Lillian drifted back into a sound sleep.

The next morning as Joseph walked into the breakfast room of Lillian's house, and from the look on Lillian's face, he knew he was in for a tough grilling. She was sitting at the small breakfast table with a cup of steaming coffee in front of her. She glanced up, waiting until Joseph poured himself a cup of coffee and sat down across from her, before she asked, "What are Chester and a deputy doing parked in front of my house?"

Joseph glanced out the window and murmured a soft curse. He had failed to tell his deputy not to park in front of Lillian's house. After taking a sip of coffee, Joseph gave Lillian a blunt answer. "There is a hit-man in town, with your name on his bullet."

Stunned, Lillian was at a loss for words for a moment, which gave Joseph time to add, "I thought we were close enough that you could have told me you were in trouble."

"I didn't want you involved, and I thought it was over, as far as my part was concerned," Lillian said, shaking her head. "God. . . what a fool I've been. Not until he is in his grave will this be over."

"Until who is in his grave," Joseph asked, knowing he was not going to like the answer.

Taking a deep breath, Lillian's answer is hesitant. "Our Texas Attorney General, Henry Winks, was one of the two silent recipients of the laundered money. One of the recipients was a non-profit foundation named "Texans for Liberty." The second recipient was a law firm called "Liberty for All." The CEO of the foundation was Winks, the CEO of the law firm was the Texas Attorney General's wife, Elizabeth."

Lillian paused for a moment, remembering back before all the chaos. Taking a deep breath, she released it slowly and continued. "When I turned the recording over to the Texas Rangers, I went into protection provided by the United States Marshall's office. Winks was arrested and released, pending trial. Winks' wife filed for divorce, claiming she knew nothing about where the money came from. Three weeks before her divorce was finalized, she was killed in a car accident. My attorney was killed in another horrible car accident. I ran and didn't stop until I met Jonathan."

Draining his cup, Joseph tried to digest what Lillian had just told him. It wasn't easy!

"Jonathan has known all along about you, and neither of you thought I should be told?" Joseph asked, his anger growing.

"We had both hoped there would be no need to ever tell you until Winks was put away," Lillian told him, and added, "We both had gotten to the point of forgetting. We were not worried about anyone coming here looking for me. Winks is due to go on trial in 30 days. There is more than enough evidence to convict him without my testimony."

"And yet there is an assassin out there with your name on his bullet," Joseph said, fighting the anger that was boiling in his gut. "Who knew where you were?" he asked, and added, "beside your contact?"

Shaking her head, Lillian knew she was about to tell Joseph something he is not going to like. "I called my sister to check on my mother." Before Joseph could tell her how dumb that was, she said, quickly, "I haven't seen my mother or sister in six years. My testimony is no longer crucial to Winks conviction. I didn't think I mattered anymore."

Joseph was slow to respond, knowing full well that yelling at Lillian at this point would do little good. "Beginning now, you go nowhere without Chester or me. Your point of destination is from home to the courthouse and back home until this guy is caught," he told her, and in a quieter tone, asked, "You understand?"

Lillian nodded, and despite the fact she was now a little scared, she smiled, telling him, "I understand."

Standing, Joseph picked up his and Lillian's coffee cups, set them down in the sink, and turned back to Lillian. "Okay, let's get to the courthouse. I want to see what Lucas has come up with?"

Slowly rising to her feet, Lillian spoke softly, tears flowing as she pleaded, "Joseph, please, you have to listen to me. These people you are going after are ruthless. They will not stop at anything to silence you. They will make you wish for death."

Walking back to stand before her, Joseph put his arms around Lillian and pulled her to him, kissing the top of her head as he told her, "I hear you, but this old Comanche didn't get long in the tooth without figuring out how to keep my scalp."

Despite being scared enough for the both of them, Lillian smiled, praying silently that the Lord above would see to it that no harm came to her savage.

CHAPTER 3

Joseph stood back against the front wall of the squad room as the company of Liberty County Deputies, all twelve of them, filed into the room and took a seat. Shutting the door behind the last deputy who entered, Joseph walked over and stood behind the podium. He introduced Lucas, who was now passing out flyers on McCain.

"Texas Ranger Lucas Wilson is passing out flyers on a fugitive who we believe is here in Liberty. He is considered armed and extremely dangerous. If you see McCain, you are not to try and apprehend him. You are to call in for assistance and observe the fugitive until backup arrives." Looking from face to face, Joseph asked, "Have you understood everything I said?"

In a loud chorus of one, they responded, "YES SIR!"

Nodding, Joseph stepped back from the podium and said, "You're dismissed. Stay safe out there."

Lucas walked over to stand beside Joseph, waiting until the twelve deputies file out. "Do you think they will spot him?"

Joseph wished he could say that they would, but he knew better. Shaking his head, he said, "No, McCain is good at what he does, or he would not have lasted as long as he has. We need to try and find out if the dead guy at the old mill was his contact here in Liberty. If not, who did he call to pick him up? That is going to be the same person who gave Lillian's location away."

After leaving the squad room, the two walked back to the sheriff's office. As they passed Lillian, who is seated next to Alice Brewer, the new dispatcher being trained to take Lillian's place, Joseph motioned for Lillian to follow him into Jonathan's office.

Once the three of them were seated, Joseph picked up the phone, punched a couple of numbers, and when he received an answer, he punched the speaker button on the phone, and says, "I have you on speaker, Jonathan. Lucas Wilson and Lillian are present."

Jonathan Lawrence's voice was sharp and crystal clear, all the way from Rome, Italy, as he said, "Joseph has filled me in on what is happening, and Sam and I are on the way home. . . should be there by noon tomorrow. In the meantime, Lucas, you and I have not met, but Joseph has spoken highly of you, and that's good enough for me. What can you tell me about who you figure is pulling the strings?"

Clearing his throat, Lucas hesitated before saying, "You understand, its only speculation at this point. I don't have any proof."

"You have any doubt?" Jonathan's words were sharp and to the point.

This time Lucas did not hesitate, "No sir, none."

"That's good enough," Jonathan assured him.

"Winks is a major cog in the scheme of things but he isn't the number one guy. Number one has always been a hidden figure, kept in the background. Politically he is out front pulling strings to make it appear he is fighting corruption, etc., for the people who elected him."

Lucas took a deep breath and released it slowly. "Hell, in for an ounce, go for the pound," as his grandma always said. "Senator Charles Abbott of Texas has his fingers in just about anything you see Winks' name on. We just can't prove it."

If Jonathan or Joseph was stunned or surprised at this

accusation, neither gave any indication.

Joseph was the first to speak. "What do you need to stick this to Abbott?"

"We need for Winks to flip and give him to us," was Lucas' answer.

Leaning back in his chair, Joseph grunted, "Humph, why didn't you say that, to begin with."

Jonathan's short laugh was attached to a warning, as he says, "You need to keep an eye on Joseph, or he'll go Comanche on you."

Not understanding, Lucas asked, "Comanche?"

"Yeah," Jonathan told him. "The Comanches were the best at getting secrets from their enemies."

Lucas' "Oh" carried a deep understanding of Jonathan's warning.

Not waiting for suggestions, Jonathan gives a curt command. "I want Winks there by the time I arrive. Bring him in!" The dial tone sounded before either Lucas or Joseph could reply.

Looking at Joseph with a slightly stunned expression, Lucas asked, "Is he always like that?"

Joseph's smile was one of complete understanding, as

he answered, "Pretty much so." Then, without hesitation, he inquires, "Where will I find Winks?"

"He's usually at his offices in Austin, or his ranch outside of Fredericksburg. Why?"

Joseph's face was grim, as he told Lucas, "You heard the Sheriff. He wants Winks here, so I'm bringing him in." Walking to the door with Sam at his heels, he paused, reached down to ruffle her fur, and looking at Lucas, said, "Keep her, and find out and text me Winks's location while I arrange a chopper."

Lucas got to his feet, questioning, "What about McCain, and why you, not me?"

"McCain is boxed in, he isn't going anywhere that George and his deputies won't be there waiting. You're the Governor's man. I'm expendable, you're not." Joseph answered. Lillian followed him, knowing that she was not going to like anything Joseph was about to tell her, but before she could question him, he told her, "Jonathan and Samantha are on their way home. I've going to bring Winks in for questioning. You are not to get out of sight of Chester and whatever deputy he has with him. You understand?"

Nodding, Lillian sighed, and said, "Yes, I understand. But, how are you going to get Winks' to come in??"

"I will convince him it's the thing to do, and you have to plan a welcome-home dinner for the bride and groom," Joseph told her, trying to make things light so as not to worry her, even though he knew it would do little good.

Lillian remained silent for several long moments, her eyes looking deep into his as though she was trying to read his hidden thoughts. Knowing it did her little good to argue with him, or to even plead with him, she gave him a swift kiss, stepped back and said, "You better not bring home any wounds that need tender loving care! You won't get it from me."

Smiling, Joseph was relieved. "Yes ma'am, I promise, no wounds."

Lillian stood and watched until Joseph exited the building. Then she turned to face Lucas, who had been watching the exchange between Lillian and Joseph and then took her anger out on him. "What is he trying to do? Get himself killed?"

Shaking his head, Lucas told her, "I don't think that would be part of his plan, but as for the rest, I have no knowledge."

Lillian wasn't sure she believed him but she knew it would do little good to continue questioning him. She could only pray that Joseph would come back alive and uninjured. Right now, all she wanted to do was plan the homecoming meal that Joseph had told her he expected her to have ready and waiting for Jonathan, Samantha, and him.

Walking back over to the dispatcher desk, she retrieved her purse. Looking at Chester and Deputy Pete Rawlings, she sighed, telling them, "Alright, you two, we are going shopping." Both deputies jumped to their feet and followed Lillian out. Getting into the back seat of the squad car, she told them, "You both can forget about following me around like sheep in the produce market. You both will wait outside, at the door if you must, but outside." She was emphatic, even more so as she added, "Outside, understand?" Both nodded that they understood.

As the deputy's car pulled off the parking lot onto the street, a late model blue Kia pulled away from the curb and followed them. A few minutes later, as the deputies pulled into the produce market parking lot, the Kia pulled into the lot across the street from the market.

Lillian, Chester, and Deputy Rawlings got out and walked up to the door. Lillian stopped and gave each of them a stern look. Both men backed up to lean against the wall next to the door, letting her know they would wait there for her return. Neither men noticed the driver of the Kia getting out of the car and walking around to the back of the store.

Once inside, Lillian forgot all about the two watchdogs waiting outside, and set about shopping for the fresh vegetables she is going to need for her gumbo and peach cobbler. Engrossed in her task, she failed to notice the store employee who walked up beside her as she is checking out the peaches, until he spoke to her.

"Ms. Marcus, you are really gonna like our peaches this week. They are really juicy and the sweetest."

Glancing at the employee and seeing his name on his store apron, she smiled, telling him, "I hope so Gerald, I am making a very special cobbler tonight."

"In that case ma'am, let me give you a sample." Gerald removed a thin, narrow-blade paring knife from his belt, and preceded to peel a peach. Then he sliced off a piece and handed it to Lillian.

Lillian took the peach slice from him, and as she bit into it, she felt a sharp jab against her rib cage as Gerald leaned closer and whispered in her ear, "Go quietly to the back, and you won't get hurt."

Her heart pounding, Lillian moved down the produce aisle, trying to keep her senses about her. She pushed open the double doors leading to the storage/warehouse area while praying someone would be in the warehouse, someone who might be able to distract her assailant. They had almost reached the back-exit door when the door to the walk-in freezer was flung open and a man with blood streaming down his face staggered out, yelling, "Help!" His scream for help brought two other store employees running, one yelling, "Call an ambulance." Lillian stopped abruptly, causing Gerald to stagger, which gave her a moment to jerk away and scream, "Help!" Uttering a harsh curse, he lunged at her. Lillian gasped as the knife penetrated deep into her side beneath her rib cage. As she slid to the floor, the knife was plunged deep into her side again. She was conscious just long enough to hear a woman scream.

Hearing the yells and screams as several employees came running through the warehouse section doors, McCain ran out the back. Jumping off the loading dock, he sprinted around the building as Chester came running out the door yelling for the young deputy with him to call for an ambulance and backup. As Chester rounded the building, he saw McCain running behind the local pharmacy toward a wooded park, directly behind it. Once McCain was in the woods, Chester knew he would have trouble following him, but he kept at a dead run, hoping the foot race would not be a waste of time when time was vital.

CHAPTER 4

Standing at the emergency room doors, Lucas and Chester and Sam turned to face Joseph as he ran in.

"She's in surgery. The doctor will give us a report as soon as he is able," Lucas told Joseph, knowing it wasn't what he would want to hear.

Taking a deep breath, Joseph asked, "What happened?"

Chester spoke first, clearly very shook up, and scared for Lillian, "We let her go in to buy some groceries. She wasn't in there no time. No one entered the store that we didn't know. The guy had to have come in through the back. He must have followed us from the sheriff's office!"

Managing to control any outburst, Joseph said, "Just tell me what's being done to catch McCain."

Lucas spoke up, bringing Joseph up to current status. "Chester chased McCain until he lost him in the woods. The Highway Patrol has closed all roads leading in and out of Liberty. The Game Wardens are patrolling the river and all the docks. The Res police are scouting the campgrounds, and choppers are scaling the timberline. He went into the woods, and so far, he has not been seen since."

The words of rage that came from Joseph were soft but easily heard and understood. Taking a deep breath, Joseph held his reply, as the surgeon walks through the swinging, operating room doors.

Dr. Charles Barton walked up to the three men, pulled off his operating cap and wiped his face with it before speaking. All three waited for him to be the first to speak.

"She was hit in one lung and in the spleen, and she's lost a lot of blood," the doctor told them, adding, "The next twenty-four hours are critical. We will know more by then."

Taking a deep breath, Joseph asked, "May I see her?"

Nodding, the doctor warned, "But only for a brief moment, and no one else."

As Joseph walked into the operating ICU unit, the nurse motioned him to Lillian's bed. Even though he was expecting the worse, Joseph was stunned at the sight of the slim form lying so still.

Joseph reached for her hand, holding it gently as he leaned forward to whisper, "Its Isatai." He wasn't sure, but if his life depended on it, he would have died swearing Lillian's fingers moved, ever so slightly. Kissing her forehead in almost a swift, warm breeze, Joseph straightened and walked out.

Lucas and Chester got to their feet as Joseph came out of the operating room, the same question on their lips. "How is she?" Shaking his head, Joseph went straight to the heart of what was eating him alive.

"McCain belongs to me. Chester will take me to where he lost him." Looking at Lucas, he asked, "Will you stay here until Chester gets back?"

"Yeah," Lucas answered, quickly, and added, "Then I'm bringing Winks in for a visit."

Joseph studied Lucas for a moment before asking, "What about the Governor?"

"I resigned, I am my own man, as of now," Joseph was told.

Chester stood silent while the two men spoke, but he had not forgotten, nor would he, that Lillian had been hurt on his watch.

"I'm staying with Lillian; no one gets near her alive unless I know them personally," he promised Joseph.

Nodding, Joseph understood exactly how Chester was feeling, and what he meant with his pledge. Turning to look back at the double, swinging doors to the ICU unit, Joseph closed his eyes for a brief moment, then turned and walked away, with Chester hot on his heels. His truck was parked in the police zone right at the Emergency exit door. Opening the car door, Joseph got in just as his cell phone rang. Removing the phone from his belt, he answered, "Skywolf." Jonathan was on the other end. Chester called him to let him know what had happened. "How's Lillian?" was his only greeting.

"She's hanging in. The doctor says the next twenty-four hours are the crucial ones," Joseph told him.

"And what are you doing?" was Jonathan's next question. Joseph did not mince words. "Going after McCain." Both men were silent for a moment until Jonathan said, "Bring him in alive if you can."

Joseph's answer was silence, as he disconnected from the cell phone. He started the truck and drove out of the hospital parking lot, not looking back.

At the edge of the woods where Chester had started his chase, Joseph got his backpack out and handed his truck keys to Chester. Reaching up, he removed his badge and handed it to Chester as well.

"Give the badge to Jonathan; he'll understand," he told Chester.

Looking down at the badge, Chester figured he knew why, as well. Joseph did not plan on bringing McCain back alive. Swallowing, Chester nodded and said, "I won't let anything happen to Lillian again. I promise."

Nodding, Joseph hoisted the backpack onto his back, whistled for Sam, and trotted off into the forest. Chester stood and watched until dog and man had disappeared from sight before he got into the truck and headed back to the hospital, saying a silent prayer for Joseph's safe return.

It was easy to pick up Chester and McCain's' clear heel prints in the crushed leaves and pine needles. Sam locked onto McCain's scent within seconds. Joseph knew he could leave the tracking to Sam's keen nose.

Two hours later, a small creek offered a rest stop and the opportunity to sip refreshing water. Sam did not bother to drink daintily from the creek edge, she jumped in with a joyful splash, and Joseph, despite the heavy load weighing on his heart, found he could not help but smile at her antics. Sitting down beneath a tall pine, Joseph leaned his head back against the trunk and closed his eyes. It would be dark soon, and he knew that McCain would stop for the night, but he and Wendy would not. It was going to be a cloudless night with a full moon, and he didn't need any more light than what would be offered. Sam would handle the rest. Hearing the cry of a raven overhead, Joseph opened his eyes and looked up at the large black bird that was floating on the wind current, slowly across the blue sky. Standing up, Joseph spoke in the ancient tongue of his ancestors, "Uncle Tuwikaa. It is good seeing you."

As though the raven understood what he said, it screamed and dove toward the earth, only to turn sharply and climb back toward the sky. Sam, who had been lying patiently while waiting for Joseph to make a move, bounded to her feet, and with a soft bark, lead off across the creek. McCain was headed north. The sun was setting, and deep shadows were forming. Joseph took off after Sam at a slow, easy lope. He wanted to catch up with McCain before daylight. With that thought, he also said a silent "thanks" for the fact that Sam was not a barker. They would be on McCain before he even knew they were close.

Chester rejoined Lucas, who was in the ICU waiting room. Both men were so engrossed in their thoughts that they both started talking at the same time. Lucas apologized first, telling Chester. "Sorry, go ahead."

Chester released a deep sigh, asking. "How's Lillian? Any changes?"

"No," Lucas told him, adding, "The doctor came out about half-an-hour ago and said she was about the same."

Reaching up, Lucas unpinned the Ranger badge from his shirt pocket and handed it to Chester, saying, "You might as well take this one, too. Give it to the sheriff for the Governor."

Studying the badge lying in the palm of his hand, Chester shook his head and said, "It's not right. You and Joseph doing this on your own."

"It's the only way, Chester. We can't take the sheriff or the Governor's offices down with us if our vigilante acts go astray," Lucas told him, adding, "Besides, vigilante law in Texas is a historical fact, so we are not the first."

"Yeah," Chester grudgingly admitted, and added, "but most of those fellows ended up getting hung. What are you planning on doing?

"Plans right now are to bring Winks in, so we can question him and not get killed doing it. Figure Joseph will do the questioning. . . might not be pretty." Giving him a lopsided grin, Lucas shook his head and asked Chester, "Where might be a safe place to stash a secret like that?"

Chester didn't like what he was about to say, but taking a deep breath, he plunged in. "The Res. Take him to the campground where McCain killed that guy. No one's going in there for a while."

"Good idea, Chester. You'll let the Indian Chief out there know that we'd appreciate some privacy?"

"Oh sure, I know George Seville is just going to love how the white man is taking over his Res," Chester told him.

Laughing, despite the seriousness of the moment, Lucas slapped Chester on the shoulder, and said, "Keep the porch light on, Chester, I'll be back."

Walking away, Lucas wasn't so sure of his or Joseph's

return, but he knew one thing was for sure, Joseph would go down in a blaze, and if he really thought about it, he figured that might not be such a bad way to go.

Driving to Austin or Fredericksburg was not out of the question, but it would take too much time. The first thing he needed to do was to find out just where Winks was today, and next, hitch a ride. Thirty minutes and two phone calls later, he was being lifted into the air by a local pilot and his jazzed-up whirlybird. Winks was at his offices in Austin, having arrived earlier that day. The helicopter landed on a small private field an hour later. A rental car was waiting, just as his friend had promised. Lucas got into the car, turned it on, and headed into the city. There would be no turning back now, not that he was thinking about turning back. Winks had been allowed too much time. . . it was time to end things.

The drive into Austin took an hour-and-a-half. He arrived just in time for the rush-hour traffic, which Lucas figured would be to his advantage. People would be rushing to get out of their workplace and home to the family. The last thing on their minds would be the possibility they might witness a kidnapping.

Lucas had done detail research on Winks. He knew, for instance, that Winks always parked on the third-floor parking building of the Bank of America, and he never came down with the first rush of escaping, five o'clock workers who were headed home. He would arrive via the elevator at exactly 6:15 P.M., drive out of the building at exactly 6:20 P.M. and head to his downtown, high-rise apartment until the dinner hour, usually eight o'clock. His helicopter would be waiting for him on the roof of the apartment building and would take him to his ranch. This was Winks routine five days a week, until the weekend and then repeat, starting his week on Monday morning.

Grabbing Winks in a busy city street, one full of people would be noticed, but it was a risk he was not willing to take. The best and smartest plan was to take Winks on the helicopter pad. Actually, removing the helicopter pilot would be easy. Subduing Winks without killing him could prove to be a heavy task. Winks was a light-weight boxer and was known to be one tough hombre.

Lucas was waiting when Winks' helicopter landed, and if things went according to schedule, Winks would be arriving in the next ten minutes. Coming in on the pilots' blind side, he waited for the door to open and for the pilot to emerge. Knowing the blow was going to be something the pilot would feel for a while, once he gained consciousness, Lucas made the blow to the back of the pilots' neck one that put him under without permanent damage. Catching the pilot as he went down, Lucas dragged him to the helicopter's cargo door. Taking a pair of handcuffs off his belt, he cuffed the pilot's hands, then removed the pilot's jacket, ripped a sleeve from the pilot's shirt, using it to gag him. He then ripped off the second sleeve and used it to blindfold the pilot; he didn't want the pilot to be able to identify him. Once the pilot was secure, Lucas took the pilot's jacket, slipped it on and set the pilot's cap down snuggly on his head. Gripping the pilot under his arms, he did a fireman's lift and hoisted him into the cargo hold, then went around and got in behind the controls. Seconds later, Winks came through the roof doors, and without a word of greeting to his pilot, climbed into the helicopter, settled back, fastens his seat belt, leaned his head back, and closed his eyes. Lucas moved the drive shaft and ascended into the skyways over Austin. It wasn't but a few moments later that Lucas was able to pick up the audible snores coming from Winks. "Now if he'll just sleep until Liberty," he said, quietly to himself.

Lucas' fondest desire was not granted. A few minutes more and Lucas could have landed without trouble, but Winks woke up, sat up, looked around and demanded, "Where the hell are we?"

Lucas spoke in a low voice, hoping to hide his Australian accent. "Bad weather, Sir. Had to take a slight detour."

Winks leaned forward, and looking out of the side window, he snarled, "I don't know what you're pulling, but you turn this bird around, now!"

With these last words, Winks started to pound on Lucas's back, causing the helicopter to take a dive. Pulling back on the stick, Lucas yelled at him, "You idiot! You'll cause us to crash!" Gripping the drive stick in his left hand, Lucas swung with his right hand and caught Winks on the side of his head. Dazed, he fell back, giving Lucas time to set the helicopter down at the Tombigbee Campsite directly below them. Lucas opened the door and jumped out, dragging Winks with him. He slammed him down on the ground, pining Winks hands behind his back. Then he fastened a pair of handcuffs on Winks he before could make any effort to fight back. He might not be making a physical fight of it, but he was yelling enough to wake the dead, never mind about anyone nearby.

With a low curse, Lucas popped Winks one more time on the jaw, knocking him out, once again. Picking Winks up beneath his arms, Lucas dragged the unconscious Winks into the nearest cabin and laid him on one of the small twin beds. Ripping the sheets off the second twin bed, Lucas preceded to tie Winks to the bed. As the unconscious Winks began to awaken, Lucas took one of the pillowcases and tied it as a gag around Winks' mouth. He took the other pillowcase and used it as a blindfold, hoping Winks had not gotten too good a look at his face. Just maybe he would come out of this with a life that wasn't behind bars. His identity and the others had to be kept secret. Standing, Lucas looked down at Winks who was struggling to get loose. Lucas knew he most likely has kissed his career goodbye, maybe even his freedom. This was one hell-of-a-mess he had gotten himself into, and right this moment, he couldn't see how he was getting out of it.

Hearing a loud shrill whistle come from out front of the cabin, Lucas peered out the window and saw a couple of Tribal deputies standing next to the helicopter. Going out to join them, Lucas wasn't surprised to see that George Seville was one of the two reservation cops. His "hell" was implicit. Walking out the door, Lucas hailed Seville and his deputy, hoping they were as friendly toward the sheriff as Chester had said they were.

Throwing up his hand in a warm salute, Lucas greeted them with, "Admiring my whirlybird, boys?"

Seville nodded, his smile lacking warmth. As he glanced toward the cabin, he let Lucas know he was not happy.

"This bird is gonna attract lots of attention from overhead, you know?"

Nodding, Lucas hurried to relieve Seville's uneasiness.

"Yeah, I'm flying it out right now. I'll drive back in to keep my friend company," Lucas said.

It was still apparent that Seville is not happy with the situation, as he asked, "The sheriff's due in today, right?"

Lucas nodded, and said, "Yes sir, he is." Glancing over his shoulder toward the cabin, he added, "The AG has no idea where he is, and I promise you he won't. Nothing will tie back to the Res."

Seville gave out a grunt of disbelief and told him, "Yeah, my ancestors believed what those white men said a few hundred years ago."

With these final words of doubt, Seville and his deputy turned and walked back into the forest, allowing Lucas to run back into the cabin to give a final check on Winks, and to assure that he was tied tight and would be there when he got back. Satisfied everything was secure, he trotted back outside. Going around to the pilot's door, he opened it and lifted his right leg to enter, only to be slammed up against the side of the chopper with a vicious blow. Before Lucas could react, he was grabbed by the neck and slung onto the ground. Rolling, Lucas jolted to his feet and whirled to face his attacker, only to be slammed backward with the jarring impact of a bullet. As Lucas falls in searing pain, and then into unconsciousness, his last thought is, "Hell, the pilot got loose!"

The strong smell of smoke penetrated Lucas' nostrils, shocking him into consciousness as he struggled to open his eyes. A sharp stabbing sensation slammed beneath his right rib cage that brought a gasp of pain. Placing his hand on the spot, he felt a warm, sticky sensation he knew to be blood. Breathing deep, he tried to sit up and felt a warm gush of fresh blood. "Damn, this isn't how I thought I would end things," Lucas muttered, as he slipped back into oblivion.

Lucas wasn't sure how long he was out, but he knew this time he wasn't alone. Opening his eyes, he waited for his vision to clear, hoping whatever was poking around in his ribs wasn't a wild animal looking for a meal. When his vision did clear, he saw that he had been moved, and a grizzled old Indian was mumbling over him as he packed Lucas' wound with tree moss. Lucas also was able to tell that the bleeding had stopped. Whatever the old guy was doing, it was working. The soft chant the old man was singing had a soothing effect, and a doziness closed his eyes.

The departure of the old man's hands brought him back to a more acute awareness, enabling Lucas to force his eyes open. The old man was gone, through a dim fog, Lucas saw only the shadow of a large gray and white canine disappear into the forest, as unconsciousness engulfed him once again.

The sensation of being lifted opened Lucas' eyes once again, and he realized he was being placed on a stretcher. He forced his vocal cords to work, uttering, "Where…. where is …the old man?"

The two Reservation deputies looked from one to the other. One deputy answered, telling him, "Sorry fellow, there was no old man that we saw."

Lucas closed his eyes, and his last conscious thought was, "Wonder what happened to the Indian?

CHAPTER 5

Standing in the deep shadows of the timberline, Joseph let his hand drop down and his fingers gently rubbed the top of Sam's head, as he spoke in a whisper. "Our friend is awake, girl. I'd say he hasn't slept much."

McCain had built a bed of pine needles beneath one of the tall pines, and from the look of his appearance, he had managed to get one or two hours of sleep.

Sam shifted her weight from one leg to the other, giving an indication of her readiness. "It's okay, girl. Let's give daylight a few more minutes," Joseph whispered to her.

The words were no more than out of Joseph's mouth when McCain stood up, dusted off his trousers, and looked around his clearing. Knowing McCain was off balance, Joseph released Sam with the command, "Take!" Without hesitation, and with a deep growl, Sam shot through the space separating her from her pray. Startled at the sound of Joseph's voice and the dog's growl, McCain whirled, pulling his revolver from his shoulder holster just as Sam hits him. The impact of Sam's body and the jabbing stab of pain he felt as her teeth bit down into the flesh of his forearm caused McCain to scream and to stumble back. The gun discharged. In a couple of strides, Joseph had McCain pinned to the ground, a knee pressed firmly down between McCain's shoulder blades.

"Hold still, or I'll turn the dog loose again." Joseph snarls.

Sam had backed off, but a steady growl and a showing of fangs had McCain lying still. Snapping the handcuffs on McCain, Joseph removed his knee, allowing McCain to roll over and sit up.

McCain recognized Joseph, and as the taste of bitter bile bit his mouth, he hurriedly offers, "I have some high-tell information. Your bosses are going to want to talk." Not waiting for a response, McCain adds, "It could be worth a lot of money and clout."

Hearing about all he could stomach, Joseph pulled out his revolver and jammed the barrel in McCain's gut, snarling, "Shut your mouth, or I will put a couple of rounds through you."

Joseph stood and walked away, taking deep gulps of air. Getting McCain back to the courthouse might prove to be more than his rage could handle. Not hearing how Lillian was doing certainly wasn't helping him to stay calm. As he turned back to face McCain, it was hard not to blow the scum's brains out, but Joseph wanted the one who paid McCain, and he needed McCain alive and talking to accomplish that. He put his gun back into its holster and took a step closer, telling McCain, "You and I are going to walk out the same way we came in. You need to understand; your life isn't worth spit right now. I had just as soon cut your throat, as not. The only reason you are alive is because of the information you have."

Walking over to stand above McCain, Joseph stared down at him, his eyes cold, as he said, "You make one wrong move, one tiny movement I don't like, and you are a dead man. My promise to you is that your death will be extremely painful. You need to keep in mind, I am Comanche."

Joseph would have almost sworn that McCain's eyes widened at the meaning of the Comanche threat. "Good," McCain must have read about the bloody history of the early Texans and the Comanche. Stepping back, Joseph holstered his gun.

"Get on your feet," he instructed McCain, and added, "we've got a long walk ahead of us."

McCain, with his hands cuffed behind him, struggled to his feet, eyeing Wendy as she faced him with a low growl still rumbling from her throat. Seeing the look McCain gave the dog, Joseph, whispered, "Good girl, Sam."

"You take the lead, and remember, if Wendy doesn't rip your throat out, I will," was Joseph's final warning, as the trek back began.

Nearing noon, Joseph called a halt. He could tell by looking at McCain that the man needed a rest stop, and, truth be told, he did too. Sitting down on the ground beneath a tall pine, McCain took a deep breath of relief. Then, after taking a refreshing drink from the water bottle Joseph held to his lips, he leaned his head back against the trunk of the tree and closed his eyes.

"You know you signed your own death warrant with this stunt," McCain told Joseph, who was sitting on a small log a few feet away, and with Wendy stretched out beside him.

Grunting, Joseph said, "Yeah, I know, but you should really think about how your boss will figure on keeping you quiet. Seems to me you're gonna be his number one concern, not me."

From the expression on McCain's face, Joseph knew the sap had not thought about his reckoning at the hands of his boss.

"You fool!" McCain screamed at Joseph, telling him, "You've killed both of us!"

Ignoring McCain's outburst, Joseph removed his cell phone from his backpack and punched in Chester's number.

"Joseph, where are you?" Chester answered on the second ring, his voice stressed.

"On the way back with McCain," Joseph told him. "Should make it to the drop-off spot by noon tomorrow."

"Have you looked at the eastern skyline?" Chester asked.

Joseph acknowledged Chester with a short, "Yeah, been watching it for about the last hour. What's the latest?"

"Well, it's not good. Weather report has the wind at

about five miles an hour but, the direction looks to be changing. Going to be coming your way from all accounts. Hopefully, the wind won't pick up that way you will most likely outrun it" Chester tells him.

"Do we need to turn around? Joseph asked.

Chester was not sure but figured better safe than sorry, so he said, "Yeah, head for the entrance to Harrigans' Swamp. I'm sending an airboat to bring you and McCain out. We're gonna need your GPS to locate you, so keep your cell phone on."

"No can do for long, battery getting low," Joseph told him.

"Turn it on when you get to the water's edge, we will find you before the battery is all gone."

"Will do," Joseph said as he disconnected, checking the time left on his phone. Then he shuts it down to conserve the remaining minutes. Clipping the phone back on his belt, he breaks the news to McCain.

"We're changing direction, and we will be moving at a slow run. Hope you're up to it."

McCain stood up, and glancing toward the rising smoke, he asked, "How much time do we have?"

Knowing there was little use in not telling McCain the facts, Joseph said, "Not enough, most likely, so we are not killing any more time; let's pick it up."

Jogging a mile is something most people can do in about twenty minutes, that is if you are healthy and able-bodied, which by this time McCain was not. The life he had been living had now caught up with him. He didn't get much rest last night and had already been trekking miles that day. McCain was not picking up much speed, and the smoke was beginning to filter through the trees and enter their lungs. Joseph did not slow the smooth easy gait, however. There was no way he planned on being fuel for a fire.

CHAPTER 6

The peaceful quiet of the town had been jarred awake by the sound of the town bell tower, the church towers, and the fire station sirens, as the dawn brought the terrifying news of FIRE! Black smoke had stretched thick fingers toward the sky, engulfing the treetops with deadly flames. There wasn't a man, woman, or child that lived in the area who did not understand the life-threatening destruction of a forest fire.

Standing at the window of the second-floor ICU unit, Chester watched the smoke, knowing there was nothing he could do but pray for those in the fire's pathway. He couldn't leave Lillian, and one more person wasn't going to make that big a difference. Hearing his name, Chester turned, as Sheriff Jonathan Lawrence and his wife Samantha walked up.

It was obvious that Chester was happy to see the sheriff. As he walked to meet him, he said, "Man, am I glad you're here!"

Shaking Chester's hand, Jonathan asked, "How's Lillian?" Chester shook Samantha's hand, welcoming her home before he faced Jonathan, telling him, "She's about the same. The Doc says she's making a fight of it. Haven't seen him yet today."

Samantha had walked over to the window during the exchange between the deputy and Jonathan, and turning to face the two men, she asked, "How bad is the fire?"

Walking over to stand next to Samantha, Chester shook his head, telling her, "The choppers have just gone up in the past minute or so. We should be getting a report soon."

Samantha turned to Jonathan and said, "You and Chester need to go. I'll stay here for Lillian. I'll call you with a report just as soon as I talk to the doctor."

Knowing it was what he had to do, Jonathan gave Samantha a quick kiss and walked out of the waiting room, with Chester at his heels.

At the sheriff's office, Jonathan changed clothes into fire-fighter gear and dialed the reservation. Seville's answer was sharp. "Jonathan, glad you're back. Have you heard from Wilson?"

Frowning, Jonathan was not sure he liked the way

things were opening up. "No, I haven't heard. Why?"

"Wilson stashed your AG at Tombigbee. Last I saw him he was going to remove the chopper and wait for you back at the cabin," Seville told Jonathan.

"And? You're telling me this because?" Jonathan knew full well the answer, even before Seville answered.

"You mean, besides me wanting your pigeon off my Res?" was Seville's response.

"Yeah," Jonathan said, adding, "what, aren't you telling me?"

"I haven't been able to raise your guy. The chopper dropped off the radar prior to the fire spotters calling in smoke, north of Tombigbee," Seville says, adding, "I've sent two of my deputies in to remove your pigeon. The fire is being pushed toward Tombigbee."

Jonathan knew that everything would hit the fan when Wink's was rescued. He also knew there was little he could do about it, for now. "Alright, bring him here," Jonathan told Seville, releasing a soft curse. "Can you tell your guys not to answer any questions from Winks? I'll handle him when they get him here."

Seville gave a short grunt of disgust, answering, "Yea,

I'll have them play dumb Indian, no speak English."

Jonathan knew Seville did not like the position he was in, but he would do as Jonathan asked, as long as Jonathan kept his end of the bargain, which Seville knew Jonathan would.

Jonathan was broken from his thoughts by Chester coming into his office. He knew by the expression on Chester's' face that something had changed. Chester didn't wait for the sheriff to speak. "The weather report just came in. Wind gusts have picked up, and the direction has changed. The fire is shifting and is moving straight at Joseph."

Standing, Jonathan walked over to his window and looked out. The smoke had gotten thicker, and it is obvious that the direction has shifted away from the town.

"Where is Joseph now?" Jonathan asked.

"South, about six clicks out. I told him to head for Harrigans' Swamp and that I'd send an airboat," Chester answered.

"How far from Harrigan's are they?" Jonathan asked.

"Couple of miles," was Chester's answer.

Turning from the window, Jonathan instructed Chester,

"You cover things here. I'll go after Joseph."

Chester had expected no less from the sheriff, and if he was truthful, he was happy that Jonathan wanted to be the one to go after Joseph. It wasn't that he was afraid of the fire catching up with him, he hated the water. The idea of skimming along the top of a swamp made him sick to his stomach. He would have been sick every minute of the journey. He did not handle the motion of a boat nor the stillness of the boat. As it sat and waited for boarding, the rocking would have him hanging his head over the side and losing the contents of his stomach.

Twenty minutes later Jonathan was on the airboat and cutting through the murky waters of the Trinity, headed toward the Harrigan's Swamp, and praying that the wind would hold.

The smoke was moving in on the swamp, making vision and breathing difficult but not impossible. Switching his GPS tracker on, Jonathan took a deep breath of relief, smoke and all. The "beep" dinged telling him he was headed to Joseph's location. Ten minutes later he saw the two men standing and waiting at the edge of the water. Slowing the boat down, he floated onto the shore and greeting Joseph with, "Glad to see you made it."

Following McCain on board, Joseph knew he had never been as glad to see anyone as he was the Sheriff, right at that moment.

"Glad to see you made it," was Joseph's reply. "Now get us the hell out of here."

Jonathan shifted into reverse and within seconds they were floating across the swamp waters, back toward the river and to safety. Glancing at McCain, who had flopped down on the floor of the boat with exhaustion, Jonathan asked Joseph, "He tell you anything interesting?"

Joseph shook his head, telling him, "Naw, didn't really have time to question him. A plus to that is I didn't cut his throat."

Trying not to smile, because he knew that Joseph's answer was exactly as he felt, Jonathan said, "Yeah, thanks for that."

Grunting, Joseph dismissed the subject of McCain to ask, "Heard from Lucas?"

"Not yet," Jonathan said. "A couple of the res deputies are going in to check on him."

Hearing the worry behind Jonathan's words, Joseph

changed the subject. "You know what started the fire?"

"According to a couple of fire rangers, a helicopter crashed," was Jonathan's answer. "They haven't been able to get in and verify as of yet. Be a while before they can."

Frowning, Joseph asked, "You don't think it was Lucas' chopper, do you?"

"Won't know until we hear from the deputies out at the Res," Jonathan said, knowing that the chances were it was Lucas' helicopter.

Before Joseph could make any reply, a jarring and violent growl erupted from Wendy, as she springs to her feet from where she was lying, and a flash of brown streaked passed both men and into McCain, who had risen to his feet without notice and was picking up a nearby hatchet. Before either Joseph or McCain could react, Sam's lung takes her straight into McCain's chest, knocking him overboard. The impact had Sam off balance, and she went over with him into the swamp. Joseph lunged for McCain and Wendy, as Jonathan killed the airboat's motor, bringing it to a stop. McCain and Wendy hit the water with a loud splash. The impact brought the marine life of the swamp alive. Alligators slid off the muddy banks into the water, and water snakes darted out and away. Leaning over the side of the boat, Joseph reached for Sam, grasping her by the collar. He pulled her back aboard as Jonathan held an oar out to McCain, who grabbed hold, allowing Jonathan to pull him in right ahead of the snapping jaws of an alligator.

"One more stunt like that and I'll let the Gators have you for their dinner," Jonathan warned McCain. Jonathan glanced from Joseph to Sam, and remarked, "Guess I know not to stack my skin up alongside the pooch, expecting a rescue from you."

Grinning, Joseph acknowledged the truth in Jonathan's statement. "Yeah, but it would be a difficult decision."

Grunting, Jonathan said, "Yeah, I believe that."

Joseph's expression darkened with renewed anger, as he glared at McCain.

"Let's get out of here and get this snake in a cell before I feed him to those gators."

No other warning was needed by Johnathan to warn McCain just how close to the line his deputy was to making his threat a reality.

CHAPTER 7

The first stop for Joseph, after arriving back on dry land, was the hospital and Lillian's' room. Walking into the ICU room, he paused for a few moments, looking at the still form. Seeing her like that was like a knife in his gut. The hot rage for the brutality of the action that put her at death's door returned. Taking a deep breath, he walked over to the bed, slowly releasing the anger. At her bedside, he leaned over placing a soft kiss on her forehead, and was surprised when she speaks in a weak voice, telling him, "You need a bath."

A big smile spread across Joseph's face, "A couple of days running around in the woods sure can place a need for one," he told her, as he moved a chair next to the bed and sat down. Taking her hand in his, he turned it palm up and placed several swift kisses on it, before scolding her. "You know you scared me out of a couple of years of my life."

Squeezing his fingers, Lillian's smile was weak as she

said, "I know, I'm sorry."

"It's okay. I promise I will give you the chance to make it up to me," he warned her.

The weak smile Lillian was able to give was evident that she was drifting off again. Giving her another kiss on the forehead, Joseph told her, "I'm going to help Jonathan get all the "I's" dotted. You get some more rest. I'll be back in a couple of hours." Lillian's slight squeeze of his fingers told Joseph she understood.

Walking out into the waiting room area, he found Jonathan waiting, and from the look on the sheriff's face, he knew something had happened.

"What's up?" was Joseph's greeting.

"They just brought Lucas to the ER," Jonathan informed him. "He's been shot."

"Damn!" Joseph responded. "What happened, do you know?"

Shaking his head, Jonathan told him, "He is unconscious. The deputies from the reservation found him and called for airlift. We'll have to wait for him to regain consciousness."

Riding down the elevator, the two were silent with

their thoughts. They stepped off the elevator, and as they walked into the ER waiting room, Joseph asked, "Do we know what happened to Winks?"

Shaking his head Jonathan says, "No. The deputies said there was no one else at the camp when they got there."

Joseph held whatever reply he was about to make, as the doctor walked out through the swinging ER doors, over to them.

"He's going to live, thanks to whoever it was that found him first and did some crude first aid," he said. "He lost a lot of blood and will be out for several hours. You can talk to him when he regains consciousness."

Nodding, Jonathan thanked the doctor, removed his cell phone from his belt and punched in his office number. When the desk clerk answered, he said, "Patsy, get a hold of Chester and have him and one other deputy come to the hospital. I want one man on Lillian's door, and the other on Lucas Wilson's door. No one goes in, no one, understand?"

Patsy Albert, the temporary replacement on the dispatch board, and longtime resident assured him she understood.

Hanging up, Jonathan told Joseph, "I'm going back to the office to get McCain settled in. Why don't you go home and get cleaned up and join me later."

Shaking his head, Joseph said, "I can take a shower at the jail. I have a change of clothes there. I'm not leaving until I know our next step."

Jonathan knew even before he gave Joseph his suggestion that there was no way his deputy would have left.

"Okay, I'll meet you back at the office." Before walking away, he added, "I spoke to Lillian's doctor. He said she had a close call but is going to be OK."

A slight smile tugged at Joseph's lips, as he shakes his head, saying, 'Yeah, I know. My girl's a tough lady."

Jonathan's smile says it all, as the two walked out of the entrance of the hospital to their vehicles, and just as Chester and the accompanying deputy drive up., Chester parked, got out of his car, and walked over to the two, to ask, "How's Lillian?"

Leaving Joseph to assure Chester of Lillian state of health, and to bring Chester up on the current status of

Lucas' health, Jonathan got in his car and drove off. Watching him drive away, Chester shook his head and told Joseph, "The Sheriff is going to rain war down on somebody's head." Looking at Joseph, he asked, "How are you handling things?"

Getting in his car, Joseph's tone was deadly, as he answered, "I'm handing it."

Watching him drive away, Chester's soft words of, "Yea, you're handing it," carried a deep warning of things to come.

Back at his office, Jonathan settled behind his desk, just as Joseph walks in. Before he could say anything, Joseph sat down in the chair opposite the desk, and in a deadly, quiet voice, said, "I want to talk to McCain."

Nodding, Jonathan told him, "I figured you would. I just came from a short, cordial meeting with him."

Leaning forward, Joseph's manner was affable, but forced, as he asked, 'How cordial?"

"Warm, not too jovial," He assured Joseph. "He is willing to testify that Winks hired him to kill Lillian, but as far who Winks boss is, he has nothing but hearsay."

Taking a deep breath, Joseph released it slowly, and

said, "McCain was the bullet. Winks, the middleman? I thought Winks was the top dog?"

"Yeah, me too," Jonathan assured him, knowing full well neither of them would rest until that jackal was behind bars, or dead, he said.

"First, we put McCain in a hole somewhere. His life isn't worth a plug nickel right now. Then we see where Winks is. To save his neck, Winks just might testify."

The phone on the desk interrupted any comment from Joseph, and from the changing expression on the sheriff's face, Joseph knew the news was not good. Hanging up, Jonathan told Joseph, "That was Seville. They found the chopper that crashed. It was Winks.' He's dead."

Too stunned to make an instant reply, Joseph let it sink in that their chances of finding the "top dog" were slim, if non-existent.

"We will have to wait for Lucas and hear what he has to say. Then make a plan of attack," Johnathan said.

"The Rangers will be investigating the chopper crash. You have any contacts that might share some details with you?" Joseph asked, hoping that there was.

"Yeah," Jonathan said, giving a brief sense of relief to

Joseph, but it was quickly taken away when Jonathan said, "Sense? Winks was or was not the top of this chain. Wonder just how far this goes?"

"Yeah, and just how does that leave the threat on Lillian?" Joseph wanted to know.

Not having an answer for Joseph was a place that Jonathan did not like being in, and he made a silent vow he would get the answers one way or another. Pushing the jail holding desk intercom number, he instructed the guard to bring McCain to his office. One way or another, he was going to end this. McCain, in handcuffs and sitting across the desk from Jonathan and next to Joseph, shifted uncomfortably in his chair, asking, "I've told you everything I know. Why am I here?"

Leaning back in his chair, Jonathan studied McCain for a few thoughtful moments. He was not sure if McCain had really told him everything, but he sure was going to find out.

"Winks is dead." He bluntly told McCain, watching for any reaction. Jonathan was not disappointed as he watched the blood drain from McCain's' face. Glancing at Joseph, he Winked and told McCain, "It looks like your boss's boss is cleaning things up to make sure nothing tracks back to him. You could be next."

McCain was obviously upset. "You got to protect me! I can't go to prison!" he told Jonathan, in a shrill tone.

Smiling an almost evil smile, Joseph asked, "Not afraid you might be the next to be shut up, are you?"

Jonathan leaned forward holding McCain's eyes, "You are bound to know more than you're saying. If you want to be stashed somewhere you might not get your throat cut, you'll talk," he told McCain, adding, "The time is now, or I'll book you and call the press."

McCain, realizing he is at the mercy of the sheriff, gave in to voice his demands. "No press, and I go before the judge, no trial, I am placed in a facility that isn't federal, with no more than 10 years for attempted manslaughter."

Before Joseph could say no, Jonathan said, "The DA will have to agree, but if you can deliver the goods, he will."

Settling back in his chair, Joseph kept his mouth shut, knowing that it was a small price to pay to get the one who was behind Winks. McCain took a deep breath and told Jonathan what little he really knew. "Winks liked his booze, and when he had the third drink his tongue loosened a little. He was tight-lipped when it came to saying the guy's name, but he'd boast that the top dog did this, or the top dog did that."

Jonathan interrupted to ask, "He never called him by his name?"

McCain shook his head. "Naw, once referred to the Democratic Senator from Texas as a top dog. I kinda figured that's who he meant when he was talking about his boss."

Before Joseph or Jonathan could make a reply, the intercom buzzed and Patsy announced, "The hospital called. Mr. Wilson is awake."

Jonathan stood and told McCain, "You're going back into your cell for a while." Then he emphasized, "We will continue this talk later."

Standing beside Lucas hospital bed, Joseph felt a knowing bit of regret for giving the young Australian a hard time when they first met.

"Doctor tells us you should be up and out of here in a couple of days," he told Lucas, only taking a second to add, "If you needed a break, there are easier ways of doing it."

Forcing a slight grin, Lucas acknowledged the truth of Joseph's jab, "Yeah, should of gone back home and left you to handle things."

Joseph's cell phone chose that moment to sound. Removing the phone from his belt, he stepped out into the hall. From the changing expression on his face, Jonathan knew whatever, or whoever was on the end of the line was not making Joseph happy. Disconnecting, Joseph walked back into Lucas' room.

"That was Seville. He just got off the phone with the feds. The FFA will be investigating the reason for the chopper crash…...they will be on site tomorrow," he told them.

Joseph looked at Lucas and asked, "You didn't do anything to that chopper, did you?"

"Hell no," Lucas told him, with underlining force on the no. Taking a deep breath, Lucas could not suppress a slight wrench, as he said, "Besides, I was about to fly that thing out and stash it somewhere. Sabotaging the chopper would make me all kinds of an idiot."

Jonathan, who had remained quiet for the last few minutes, spoke up, saying, "The feds are going to find it was an accident. Winks and his pilot were either killed in the crash or the fire. Either way, you two will be in the clear."

Joseph nodded, and said, "That leaves McCain and our Top Dog. How do you suppose we proceed?"

All three answered in sync, "Cautiously."

CHAPTER 8

Every morning for the past two mornings Lillian had awakened to see Joseph dozing in the chair beside her bed. Whether he had spent the night or just arrived early, she did not know, for he would not answer her question. He wanted her to keep guessing. The thing was, Joseph figured once Lillian could answer her own question because she was alert enough to know when someone came into her room, she would then be able to go home. Home with him, he wanted that understood as well.

As Joseph opened his eyes, Lillian smiled, telling him, "You really need to go home at night to get some real rest."

Leaning over her, Joseph kissed her forehead, saying, "Good morning to you too." Sitting down on the side of her bed, he assured her, "I rest just fine in my bed-chair, thank you."

Knowing it would be useless to push him, Lillian changed the subject, asking, "When am I going home?"

"Today," he told her, but added, "My house, not yours"

She opened her mouth to argue, but closed it just as fast, knowing it would do little good to argue the point. The main thing was, she wanted out of the hospital, period. So instead of arguing the point, she changed the subject, asking, "What has happened with McCain?"

"Jonathan delivered him to the Huntsville pen, yesterday. He's checked in there under an alias until we figure it's time to put him in the headlights. McCain's attorney and the judge worked out a deal." Joseph told her.

Sighing, Lillian felt the heavy weight of apprehension descending back onto her shoulders.

"I thought with Winks dead and McCain in custody, this would have all been over. What's our next step?" she asked, with no small amount of dread.

"Well, based on what McCain was able to tell us, we have a pretty good idea who is the big man, or Top Dog, as Winks called him." Joseph was not too sure himself what the next step was going to be, but one thing he did know, as he silently promised himself, there would be an end to the threat Lillian was living under.

"But, you are to think only of getting your strength back, or you will see my next step of action," he warned her.

Despite the seriousness of the moment, Lillian had to smile as she let him know just how concerned she was with his threat by punching him on the arm, telling him,

"You don't scare me. Now I've seen enough of your face this morning; go to work."

Kissing her softly on the lips, Joseph whispered "bye," and went in search of the head nurse to let her know Lillian was checking out today, regardless of what the doctor thought.

Despite his attitude of my way or the highway, Joseph was glad that the doctor was in agreement with Lillian's checking out. He would be able to pick her up around two that afternoon, which gave him some time to talk with Lucas and Jonathan. Both men were in Jonathan's office. Joining them, he was greeted with "how's Lillian," and once he had assured both of them that she was fine and was going home from the hospital that afternoon, he was able to ask the one big question.

Looking at Jonathan, he asked, "You come up with a plan of action yet?"

"No, but Lucas has," Jonathan said, only to question

the sanity of it all. "If our guy is who McCain thinks he is, Lucas might just get us all killed for sure this time."

"Maybe, maybe not, but this guy is going down, one way or another," was the dire warning Joseph gave.

Lucas nodded his understanding and agreement, telling them, "The Governor wants me back ASAP. He sent the Rangers to empty Winks' office, and he wants me to fine toon everything brought in before some Judge forces him to release all records back to the Senate judiciary. Right now, Winks is not missing or known dead, but once the remains of that chopper fire are made known, it will be Nellie bar the door."

"If you are going to Austin, I'm coming with you," Joseph informed the two. Before either could reply, he asked Lucas, "What do you know about Senator Abbott?"

Figuring it would be a losing argument trying to convince Joseph it was the wrong move for him to go to Austin with him, Lucas gave him what little he knew.

"Abbott is around 55, stands about 5'11", has gray hair, blue eyes, married, no children, been a senator for the Democratic party for the past eight years. He is up for re-election, and according to the polls, is considered a shoo-in."

Knowing full well this isn't the kind of information Joseph was looking for, Lucas went on to add, "Visit five minutes with his wife and you'll find out he is the perfect husband. Of course, he would be, his wife is the one holding the purse strings as far as the public is concerned. Privately you could wonder."

It was obvious that Lucas was warming up to the subject. "I figure Abbott is waiting until he is out of office to shed the shackles of matrimony, which could be this election. Maria Abbott inherited a chain of high dollar restaurants ten years ago. At the time, the chains' financial stability was weak and seem to be sinking, that is until Senator Abbott took over. Two years later, the finances were back on solid ground and even showing a small profit. Everyone agreed then that the new Senator Abbott was a smart businessman, as well as a great Senator."

Leaning back in his chair Jonathan interrupted to ask, "Is that when Abbott's trips to Mexico started?"

Nodding, Lucas said, "He didn't really start anyone looking at him until he opened one of his wife's restaurant in Sinaloa."

Jonathan injected, "The cradle of Mexico's drug trafficking?"

'Yeah, the only reason I was told to start looking into Abbott's activities is because he has made several trips to Mexico as a guest on one of the old established families. The Governor was approached by our Vice-President to see if he could help find out just what Abbott is involved in. Everything seemed very public, very open, with many foreign guests coming in and out. Some of these guests had paper trails that lead back to Afghanistan and the Papaver Somniferum, the opium poppy. The opium trade is blooming in Mexico and Abbott is a welcome politician there."

Joseph had remained quiet, listening to Lucas and digesting what was being said. Shaking his head at the magnitude of it all, he asked, "So you are telling us that the poppy from Afghanistan is being brought into Mexico where it's is being refined into opium and sold in the states?"

"That's what I am saying. Abbott is involved in laundering the money," Lucas answered Joseph, adding, "With a restaurant, you deal in cash, so you have a full house, swinging parties, and a week's deposit can be in the thousands. And since your income has jumped, you feel obligated to give. So, you know of this foundation that donates and gives around the world, so, you drop a few thousands. The foundation then gives the money to deserving people, groups, and non-profit businesses. It got the money washed clean and dispersed."

"Damn, don't know if I will be eating at any more McDonalds," Joseph responded.

Jonathan agreed, but defended McDonalds by saying, "Don't believe you need to worry about McDonalds; too many of these guys kids and grandkids eat there."

Lucas nodded his understanding, "You are not far off. A fast-food chain has, I know, been looked at, but you are right that these guys protect their kids and grandkids."

Joseph was tired of waiting for Lucas' great plan. "So, what are our next steps?"

"I'm heading back to Austin tomorrow to go through Winks files before the autopsy results come in. There is really nothing you can do until we make the next move." Lucas told Joseph.

Joseph knew Lucas was right, and the main thing for

him right now was Lillian. His time would come once he had Lillian on her feet.

Jonathan, knowing what was most likely running through Joseph's mind, decided to try and lighten the load. "When you pick Lillian up from the hospital, take her out to my ranch. My foreman and his wife, Molly, are there twenty-four seven and can be there for her. If you plan on being involved in Abbott's take-down, you are going to need help with her."

Opening his mouth to say "no," Joseph stopped. The sense of what Jonathan said was not something he could ignore. Nodding, he accepted, saying, "It's a good idea, thing is to get Lillian to agree."

"Yeah," Jonathan said, adding, "Don't envy you that."

As it turned out, Lillian did not give Joseph a hard time about staying at Jonathan's ranch, not as much as he had expected. Joseph also knew that Lillian was not liking the fact that he was leaving her to go join up with Lucas and do whatever they had to do to bring Abbott down.

Sitting across the breakfast table from Lillian in the small sunroom off the kitchen at Jonathan's, Joseph slowly sips a cup of hot coffee, waiting for Lillian's response to his announcing his departure.

Lillian was doing her best not to scream at Joseph. Trying to remain calm, and knowing that regardless of what she said, he was going after Abbott with a vengeance.

Setting her coffee cup down, she took a deep breath and released it slowly, telling him, "I have lived in dread for too many years to try and talk you out of doing this."

Getting up, Lucas walked around the table, took Lillian by the hand and pulled her to her feet. Putting his arms around her, he told her, "I will let you henpeck me for all of our married life, which is to happen as soon as Abbott is put away." His lips silenced her before she was able to speak. A long, sinuous kiss wiped all thought of Abbott from her head. As her body molded to his in warm surrender, Joseph forgot about Abbott as well.

CHAPTER 9

Looking out over the Austin skyline from the office of the Texas Attorney General, Joseph felt the old sensation of his skin crawling up the back of his neck. Turning around to face Lucas, he voiced the doubt that had been bothering him the past few days.

"Winks was too smart to leave anything lying around that would prove useful to the law. So why are we crawling through all of his thousands of pages of the past twenty years of his life?"

"Because," Lucas said, smiling at Joseph and waving a villa folder, a big smile splitting his mouth. "Winks didn't believe in the 21st-century technology."

Opening the folder, Lucas spread the newspaper clipping out, reading one aloud.

"May 2009: El Paso, Texas: Juliet Bedford, and her husband, Henry, a detention officer in El Paso, Texas, were ambushed after leaving a children's birthday party in downtown El Paso. Their SUV was sprayed with bullets, their eight-month-old daughter was found screaming in the back seat."

Joseph reached over and picked up another clipping, reading,

"July 2010: Dallas, Texas: Ralph Valence was gunned down as he stepped outside the church to smoke a cigarette after, his sister's wedding ceremony. Three men invaded the courtyard, forced the wedding party to the ground then kidnapped the groom, and his brother. They two men were, tortured and shot, their bodies later found in the city garbage dump."

"What the hell connection did Winks have with these two cases? And what were these people to him?" Joseph asked, pretty sure he knew the answer already.

Shaking his head, Lucas told him, "My time with the Governor didn't begin until 2012. I'm not familiar with the names, but I sure as hell know where to find out."

An hour later, Joseph and Lucas walked into the office of Retired General Pete Mullins, Homeland Security Advisory Council Member. Mullins, sixty-four years old, standing six feet and a hundred and ninety-seven pounds of coiled steel, rose to greet Lucas with a hearty, "Damn,

Lucas, you sure know how to stir a pot of coal."

"You taught me well, General," Lucas said as he met Mullins' firm grip. Pointing to Joseph, he introduced the two men. "Meet Deputy Sheriff Joseph Skywolf from Liberty, he's the one I told you about."

Shaking Mullins' hand, Joseph acknowledged the fact Lucas had also spoken of Mullins. "It's an honor to meet you, Sir."

Motioning to the chairs across from his desk, Mullins invites the two to sit. "I know you boys have something gnawing at your gullet, so, let's get at it."

Lucas took the lead with a pointed question, "What do you know about the killings of Ralph Valence and Henry Bedford?"

Mullins sat back in his chair, the warmth of his eyes turning suddenly cold, the lines of his jaw tightening. It was several moments before he made any reply, and when he did, he answered with a question. "What are you looking for?"

Joseph took the point this time. "We know it was drug related, and we know Texas Attorney General Winks was connected with it in some way."

"Bedford was Winks' first cousin. He was also Senator Abbott's' chauffeur. The police have never been able to figure out a motive; the guy was squeaky clean." Mullins paused a moment before acknowledging, "What I tell you two stays in this office, understood?"

Joseph and Lucas both nodded, as Mullins continues. "The common belief is that Bedford was killed to open up Abbott's' chauffer position. The wife was just collateral damage. The new chauffeur is Steven Norris, an up and coming nephew of Louis Morales, the aspiring State Representative from Colorado, who was handpicked and primed by Abbott."

Joseph was beginning to grow antsy. This was taking too long a road leading to a climax. If Abbott was the man they were after, he needed to know now.

"Senator Abbott has been on a fed watch list for the past ten months from what I understand. What happened that put him on it?" he asked, no longer willing to waste time.

Mullins smile was one of understanding, and he answered just as bluntly as Joseph question had been asked. "Valances' little sister didn't care for the way her brother was shot down. Seems she's the sweetheart of one of the cartel's top dog's son, and she is also the niece of Abbott's wife."

"So, who gave the hit on the chauffeur?" Lucas asked, with a knowing suspicion growing in his gut.

"We think, Morales," was the answer Mullins gave, adding, "If it was, he screwed up, royally!"

"So, Morales has the current chauffer killed? In order to put his nephew in a position of what?" Joseph questioned.

"That's the question currently being pondered," Mullins said, but added, "Want to hear what I think?"

Both Joseph and Lucas answered with a resounding "yes." Mullins didn't need any other encouragement.

"Abbott is becoming a liability," Mullins said, continuing, "The cartel does not like all the attention they are getting from the feds since Abbott has begun to show a remarkable interest in vacationing in Mexico."

"They are going to make a play to get rid of Abbott?" Joseph asked as he hazards a guess.

Nodding, Mullins agreed, "Yep, that's the main thought right now. But the powers that be do not want that to happen. They need Abbott alive, to turn evidence. But, to bring him down a lot more evidence is needed, and I have a feeling his time is running out."

Lucas leaned forward to ask, "What do you think it would take to get Abbott to flip?"

Mullins short laugh told Lucas just what he thought of the idea, but he gave him what he needed to hear.

"Complete immunity, to begin with, and a lifetime of protection, which means a new identity," was his answer.

Joseph took a deep breath, released it slowly before he let the two men know just what he thought of that idea. "Abbott is known far and wide. There can be no new identity."

Lucas nodded, agreeing with Joseph, but ventured a solution for Abbott's identity problem. "He could have plastic surgery. Think he would agree to that?"

"Hell, yeah!" Mullins told him, adding, "The man would do anything to stay alive. Wouldn't you?"

"The worst is yet to come," Lucas injected, adding, "A recent shooting in Chicago has the feds going a little crazy. They are fearing an all-out war between the Cartel and the MS13.

Shaking his head, Joseph knew he was not going to like what was to follow. "For a few years, now, I have lived a life of relative peace. Arrested a few drunks, domestic disturbance, a few head of cattle stolen, illegal hunting, maybe a break-in or two. Now we're talking gangs and Mexican drug lords.

"The MS13 are no ordinary street punks. They are a vicious bunch of illegal aliens that will kill your baby to show you who's king of the hill. Or, for that matter, they'll kill your whole family," Mullins told Joseph, wanting to make sure Joseph understood how serious the threat was.

"So, why are the two going to war?" Lucas asked.

"It's a turf war, "Mullins answered. "The cartel is not liking the fact these gangsters are coming into their territory. The MS13 are not your snot nose street punks trying to be king of the hill. They are as bad as Isis, or any Taliban."

"I understand our Senator is crossways with the Cartel, but how did he connect with this MS13?" Joseph asked.

"Well, the Senator has jumped on the get rid of illegal aliens bandwagon, and has personally seen to it that a couple of the MS13 members were deported," Mullins said, adding, "The big boys have to protect their soldiers, so, the word is, a hit has been put on the Senator; a flat million bucks."

A sharp, shrill whistle from Lucas was evidence of his impression of the MS13. "I'd say that gives the Senator another powerful reason to want another identity. Wouldn't you?" He inquired.

"Yeah," Mullins said, but with a slight snarl, snaps, "but what is it going to take to get him that scared? He believes he is untouchable. His security is x-military."

Joseph didn't like the direction his brain was traveling, but he was past worrying about anyone but Lillian, and he was going to see to it that Abbott paid.

"There are ways to make him see the light." Joseph stood, held his hand out to Mullins, and said, "We appreciate your help, Mr. Mullins, but from here on, I believe you should be excluded from any talks."

Mullins stood, shook Josephs' hand, and agreed. "You try and stay alive."

Nodding, Joseph answered with a lopsided grin and a firm promise. "I plan on doing just that."

Following Joseph out, Lucas inquired, "Just what are

you thinking?"

"I'm thinking I am going to hit Abbott where it will hurt the most," Joseph informed Lucas with a voice cold and hard. He added, "In his pocket!"

Lucas waited until they were seated in their cab for the ride back to the airport before asking, "How do you plan on doing that?"

Shaking his head, Joseph cut a sheepish grin at Lucas, and told him, "Not sure just yet; give me a couple of minutes."

Laughing, Lucas told him, "Oh, you can have more than a couple of minutes. Take as much time as you want. I am not eager to get myself killed."

In the chopper, Joseph settled back, closing his eyes. It would be a short flight to Liberty, but it would give him the quiet time he needed to sort out the coming events. Lucas, on the other hand, was wide-eyed and having a difficult time in not bombarding Joseph with a hundred and one questions. In his imagination, Lucas knew how he would get Abbott to talk, but he was equally sure he would have a hard time smuggling the man into Australia where some friends of his would be able to extract all the information needed. Leaning back in his seat, Lucas closed his eyes, and the hum of the rotary blades of the chopper helped him to drift off into a deep sleep.

An hour later, Joseph was waking him......they had landed. Sitting up, Lucas unbuckled his seat belt, mumbling, "Ride too damn short."

Opening the chopper door, Joseph jumped out, chastising Lucas. 'You've gotten soft working for the Governor. Need to get back on the rodeo circuit."

Joining him on the ground, Lucas had to agree but was not going to give Joseph the satisfaction of telling him so. Instead, he changed the subject by asking,

"You let the sheriff know we were coming in?"

"Yeah," Joseph said, but added, "he had already gotten a call from your boss who has spoken with our friend Mullins."

"Hell, that was quick!" Seeing Joseph's question even before it was spoken, he told him, "Mullins picks his sides carefully. He most likely feels he said too much to us. So, he is verifying our trust."

"What about our trust in Mullins?' Joseph inquired, with a touch of sarcasm.

"As far as I know, the Governor trusts Mullins as a man of integrity," Lucas told him, but he had a question. "What did you not like about Mullins?"

Waiting until they were on the road back to the courthouse, Joseph was not sure exactly what had put the arrow of caution in him when dealing with Mullins, but he knew not to distrust the feeling. Too many times it had saved his scalp.

"Mullins doesn't dislike Abbott as much as he is jealous of him. He could be giving us a slanted view," Joseph answered.

"Jealous?" The fact that Lucas was stunned by Joseph's answer did not come as any surprise. Joseph knew Lucas had had previous dealings with Mullins and had been given no reason to distrust the man, but for Joseph, he had only his instincts to go on, and he trusted them.

Arriving back at the sheriffs' office, the first thing Joseph did was to call Lillian. The sound of her voice when she answered lifted his spirits, and his "I can handle anything" attitude.

"I just got to Jonathan's office. How are you?" Voicing his main concern, Joseph held his breath, waiting for her answer.

"I am fine, now that you are back." The sound of relief in Lillian's voice was evident.

"You listening to Molly, and doing as she tells you?" Joseph knew the answer to his question even before he asked it, but he wanted to hear Lillian say it, even if it most likely would be a little, white lie.

"Yes, I am listening to Molly." Hoping to reassure him, she added, "Molly is taking wonderful care of me."

Joseph released his held breath, realizing that Jonathan and Lucas were waiting. He quickly let her go, and said, "I'll be there in an hour or so. Tell Molly I'd love some of her fried chicken."

Lucas and Jonathan interrupted what they were saying as Joseph entered the office. Jonathan quickly brought him up to date.

"Lucas told me about your meeting with Mullins, and after my talk with him, I am inclined to agree with you. He may have given a slanted view of how he sees things, but that doesn't make him wrong."

"No, that doesn't make him wrong," Joseph said, agreeing with Jonathan. "But, I am inclined to think he is."

Lucas' frown deepened, as he inquired of Joseph, "Why?"

"Well, I don't think the cartel is all that disenchanted with our guy," Joseph told him. "The cartel doesn't want the MS13 cutting into their turf, and Abbott is their main line of resistance. If Abbott gets rid of the MS13, he is going to be the cartel's fair-hair boy. And they could really care less if it causes a bloodbath here in the states."

Not wanting to agree, Lucas ventured his own thoughts. "Abbott got where he is on his wife's money. What do you think would happen if that money was taken away?"

It did not take Joseph but a couple of seconds for a light to go on in his brain, and he liked his answer. "He would need funds, so, he would have to draw from his off-shore, hidden account," he said, with a small amount of glee.

Jonathan had been sitting back listening to the two with a growing amount of respect. He had let them talk it out and had offered none of his thoughts, but now he had a question, and he was eager to see how the two would answer.

"What about trying to get Mrs. Abbott to turn on her

husband?" he inquired.

Both Joseph and Lucas looked at him with their question evident on their faces. Jonathan did not need to wait for their question, before he answered, "Sam tells me there is not a woman living who does not know her husband is cheating. They choose not to acknowledge it."

Lucas was still not sure he was understanding the sheriff's point, so, he asked, "What, we just up and tell her she needs to fess up and help nail his hide to the barn door?"

"Something like that," was Jonathan's reply. "Most women, exception Hilary, do not stand alongside the cheating rat if it becomes front page news."

Joseph was quicker to catch on to the sheriff's thinking. "So, we sic the newspaper on her and see how crazy she might become? We just happen to know a good reporter that might want to be the first to interview the lady. Right?"

Nodding, Jonathan knew he might not have so willing a reporter as he would like to believe, but he also knew there was no way Sam would not help.

CHAPTER 10

Jonathan was proven right, and even though it was against her better judgment, Sam stood at the front door of Senator and Mrs. Abbott's rambling ranch house two days later. She was surprised when the lady herself answered the door, welcoming her inside. Seated on the veranda, sipping a cup of freshly made coffee poured by her hostess, Samantha, for the first time in her career, was not so sure what question to start with. So, instead, she chose to walk softly with, "You have a lovely home, Mrs. Abbott."

Maria Abbott's slight smile was tepid as she looked around the veranda's yellow rose vines and the purple wisteria vines. Her acknowledgment of the compliment had less warmth.

"Thank you. This was the Senator's vision. I would have preferred something with fewer blooms and more greens." Realizing how she must sound; Maria quickly changed her tone. "But he is home so seldom, I want him to enjoy his time, and having the lovely plants of his choice is such a small thing to give him."

Seeing an opening, Samantha nodded in agreement, saying, "I certainly understand, and I know it must be difficult for you with the Senator being gone so much. Do you keep busy by being involved in running your beautiful restaurants?"

"Oh, no, no! That's gotten far beyond my abilities. The Senator is totally responsible for all that." Maria was quick to add, "But, I am very busy with my ladies' organizations and my charities."

To feel a little pity for the Senator's wife was not something Samantha had thought about, so, she asked, "Your father started the restaurant business, didn't he?

Nodding, Maria's smile was full of warmth this time, as her memories of her father returns."

"Yes, The Casa Maria was daddy's idea. He never dreamed it would be more than the one."

Now that Maria was warming up to the interview, Samantha did not want to lose the momentum. "That's the original one, located in New York, right?"

"Yes, yes, it was. Daddy was so proud. The Mayor and the Governor were his special guests. We had a packed house," Maria told her.

"I know you were all proud. As you must be now with so many beautiful Casa Marias located in so many lovely places, such as Mexico, and now Vegas." As Samantha was laying on the praise, she watched the light in Maria's eyes dim.

Taking a sip of what must now be tepid coffee, Maria seemed to gather her words carefully.

"Yes, yes, of course, I am proud of the Senator, but I miss the closeness of our friends that came to dine in our Casa Maria."

In for a penny, in for a pound, as her mama used to say, Samantha launched her first arrow of truth.

"Mrs. Abbott, I am sure you have heard some of the questions being asked about the Senator's travels to Mexico. Would you answer just a couple of question from me, to set the whispers to rest?"

Maria was suddenly very still, and she seemed to draw a curtain of protection about her. Never-the-less, she gave a nod of agreement.

"What made the Senator decide to open a restaurant in Mexico?" was Samantha's first question, hoping there would be a chance to ask more.

"The Ambassador Phillip Vasquez spoke to the Senator many times about opening a Casa Maria in his country. He assured the Senator that it would mean so much in forming many business ties to our two countries," Maria told, her adding, "The restaurant has done magnificently. I am very proud of the Senator."

The thought of "why did Maria Abbott keep referring to her husband as the Senator" kept skipping around in her head. It was becoming very distracting.

Samantha latched onto the one thing that Maria had said so far that was of interest, so, she asked, "What types of business interest was the Ambassador referring to?"

Clearly flustered, Maria folded her hands in her lap, and answered, "Oh, that I am not aware of. The Senator never discusses that sort of thing with me."

Leaning forward, Samantha asked, "Mrs. Abbott, are you going to the opening of the new restaurant this weekend?"

Shaking her head, Maria stood up, her answer sharp, "No, I never go to the openings anymore. The Senator is much too busy to be bothered with me at those things. It's not like it was with the first opening. Now if you will excuse me, I think this interview is over."

Standing, Samantha shook her head and said, "I am sorry if my question upset you."

"No. no, your question did not upset me. I am just not good with sitting so long," Maria offered as an excuse.

Glancing out toward the courtyard and the stables, Samantha asked,

"Perhaps we could take a walk? You could show me your stables. I understand you are quite the equestrian."

Samantha breathed a small sigh of relief when Maria's face lit up. It was obvious that the horses were her one true interest.

Walking beside Maria, Samantha kept quiet, as the senator's wife began to speak, "I wanted to be involved with all the Maria restaurants, but…." With a more scathing tone, she said, "the Senator told me things were so very different in today's world of business. Not like when I was five, and daddy opened the first one."

Stopping to stroke the nose of a beautiful bay thoroughbred, Maria introduced the filly. "This is Rosie-lee-rose. She is thirteen years old. I've had her since she was just three weeks old. Her mama died giving birth and I bottle-raised her."

Stroking the nose of the sweet-tempered mare, Samantha knew at that moment she was about to make a big mistake, as she asked, "Mrs. Abbott, are you aware that there are whispers about the type of businessmen in Mexico that your husband is dealing with?"

Clearly startled, Maria asked, sharply, "What are you talking about?"

"I'm talking about the Cartel; about Afghanistan and the Papaver Somniferum, the opium poppy. The opium trade, which is blooming in Mexico. These drug Lords are welcome in your restaurant and are made welcome by your husband."

Stunned, Maria stared at Samantha, her voice rising in reproach, "That is a lie! The Senator would never have anything to do with drug deals or drugs! You need to leave. Now!"

Samantha knew it would do little good to try and calm Maria Abbott down, but she tried, anyway.

"Mrs. Abbott, I am telling you the truth. It is not just whispers. If you will let me, I will show you what I know."

"No! Get out! Get out now!" she screamed at Samantha.

Trying to quieten Maria was doing little good, but Samantha knew she had to try.

"Mrs. Abbott, you must listen. Your life could be in danger. You could be killed!"

Samantha wasn't sure if it was her words or her tone, but with a blink of an eye, Maria Abbott seemed to become calmer, as she asked, "What are saying? The Senator would have me killed?" Maria asked with no sign of the previous hysteria.

As far as Samantha was concerned, that question was asked with entirely too much calm.

"Maybe not the Senator, but the men he is dealing with. Mrs. Abbott, I do not come to you without some knowledge of what I am telling you."

Maria Abbott was quiet for several minutes, and Samantha knew she had to let the woman have her time. She needed time to think about what had been said, and time to think and remember back about things her husband might have said, or done, in front of her that made her have a growing distrust. With a sudden shake of her head, Maria turned and started back to the house, telling Samantha, "Come, we are going into my study and you are going to tell me whatever it is you think you know."

Stopping, she turned and looked directly into Samantha's eyes, and warned,

"You had better be up front and truthful, or I promise you, you will be sorry."

This, Samantha had little doubt of. The woman Samantha had begun to feel compassion and sympathy for had utterly vanished in front of her. Maria Abbott was not a timid little soul.

An hour later, Samantha sat quietly in front of Maria Abbott's desk waiting for Maria to finish absorbing what she had just been told. Looking around the room, Samantha would have known this was Maria Abbott's study even if she had not been told. The furnishings were of walnut design, and the bookshelves lining the walls were filled with history and historical publications. Maria's desk was also walnut, and was slim, with only two desk drawers. A telephone, calendar, and a picture of the Senator were the only things cluttering her desk. As far as Samantha could see, Maria Abbott was not a piece of fluff to be hanging onto a husbands' arm. She was willing to bet Marias' daddy had taught her how to stand on her own two feet.

Taking a deep breath, Maria leaned back in her chair, closed her eyes for only a moment, and then leaned forward, resting her arms on her desk. Her attitude was one of conviction, as she asked, "So what does your husband, the Sheriff, plan on doing?"

A smile tugged at the corners of Samantha's mouth, as she responded, "Actually, you are going to get to work with Deputy Joseph Skywolf on this."

"Skywolf?" Maria was not at all sure she liked the sound of what just happened.

It did not take Maria but a few minutes of talking to Joseph over the telephone speaker, with him filling her in on what they knew and suspected, for her to know this Indian did not like the Senator. In fact, she figured Joseph would like to revert back to the actions of some of his ancestors and scalp the great Senator Abbott. If he did, it would be with her blessings.

"The sheriff's lovely wife tells me that there is a plan somewhere in all of this, a plan to expose the Senator as the slimy rat that he is. I would like to hear that now." From the tone of Maria Abbott's voice, Joseph knew the woman had a tight grip on a short rope.

"We have to flip the Senator. We need information on the Cartel, as well as the MS13, that he has. In order to do this, we have to put him in fear for his life. He has to ask for protection." Sam watched the changing expressions on Maria Abbotts' face as Joseph informed her of what they wanted to do in order to bring her husband to justice.

"We need you to remove the purse strings and to shut him down as publicly and as loud as you can. The grand opening of your new restaurant in Las Vegas would be the starting point. We have to force him to use funds he has in offshore accounts. The drug Lords have to start questioning his ability and to question if he is a threat to them."

Whatever it was that Sam was looking for in Maria's face, she did not find it. It was as though the woman was listening to a calm, clear, sun-shiny day weather report. There was no outrage or hurt, but the response received was surprising. Taking her cell phone from her purse, she punched one number, and when she spoke, her voice was cool and calm.

"Benjamin, its Maria Slaughter."

From the expression on her now expressive face, whoever the Benjamin was on the other end must have asked of her wellbeing, as she said, "I am fine, Benjamin, thank you for asking. I have something I need you to take care of for me."

Without seeming to take a breath, she told him, "Effective immediately, the Senator's signature is to be removed from all my holdings. You are to serve papers on him at the grand opening of the restaurant in Vegas that bars him from ever stepping foot on any of my properties."

Glancing at Sam, she gives a small smile, adding one last piece of instruction.

"Please see to it that the Senator is served these papers thirty minutes into the grand opening, and then he is to be escorted off the premises. I know you have questions, but I am not going to answer them at this time. I will see you at the opening and answer your questions after my gift to the Senator is given. Thank you, Benjamin."

Maria disconnected, not waiting for a response from Benjamin. Smiling at Sam's astonished face, she said, "My father did not raise no fool. I have allowed the Senator the wealthy Southern gentleman life because I felt he was doing good things for our country and our state. I also knew he was an astute businessman and made me lots of money."

Maria's tone of voice changed into pure ice as she added, "I did not know some of that was from dirty drug money."

Listening on the phone, Joseph understood where the lady was coming from, but he also understood she had just put herself in harm's way,

"Mrs. Abbott, I admire your fast action, but maybe you should think about it a little more," Joseph told her, and added, "If your husband is what we think he is, and from what we know about his associates, you could have put yourself in the line of fire."

Maria was silent for a moment, but finally shaking her head, she told Joseph,

"Then I am not going to help matters any by showing up in Vegas and shutting this grand opening down before it can get started."

Lucas, who was with Joseph listening to the exchange

between Joseph, Sam and the Senator's wife, was enjoying Joseph's uncomfortable position, but he did also appreciate his concerns. "Joseph's right, Mrs. Abbott. Maybe you should stop your attorney from carrying out those instructions."

Shaking her head, Maria smiled at Sam, and then told them all, "No, I am going to have fun with that SOB. Now I am assuming both of you young men are going to be my escort to the hootenanny?"

Stunned, the two were quick to assure Maria that they would be delighted to be her escort, and all the time Joseph was saying "yeah, sure!" he was hearing Lillian in his ear asking him if he had lost his mind.

CHAPTER 11

Driving up in front of the new restaurant in Las Vegas, Lillian's words were still ringing in his ears. "Are you out of your mind? She'll get you both killed!" Taking a deep breath, Joseph released it slowly and stepped out of the car, as the uniform doorman opened the car passenger side doors.

Seeing who was getting out, the doorman's face broke into a big smile, greeting Maria, "Ms. Abbott, so wonderful to see you. The Senator did not tell us you would be attending."

Maria Abbott's smile was warm, as she returned the greeting, "Thank you, Henry, it is good to see you again. The Senator did not know I was coming. I wanted it to be a surprise."

"And so, shall it be. The Senator has not yet arrived, but his V.I.P. guests have. Shall I arrange for the maître d' to introduce and seat you and your guests at their table?"

Maria glanced at Joseph and Lucas, her smile widening

as she answered the doorman, "Absolutely, Henry."

Henry was quick to arrange the introduction to the maître d', who, in turn, introduced Maria to the Senator's special guests, which, in turn, she preceded to introduced her "friends."

"Gentlemen, I would like for you to meet, on my left, Special Investigator for the Governor of Texas, Lucas Wilson, and on my right, Deputy Sheriff of Liberty County Texas, Joseph Skywolf. It is regrettable that I will not be able to introduce Deputy Skywolf's fiancé, Lillian. Sadly, Lillian was wounded by some lowlife knife-wielding scum, but she is just doing great."

The men acknowledge the introductions, but it was evident that they were uncomfortable and agitated. Maria seemed unconcerned with the men's state of mind, as she sat down still talking. "I'm sure you gentlemen are aware of the Senator's financials, otherwise you would not have traveled so many miles to be here at this small opening."

Any trace of humor vanished from Maria's face, as she lowered her voice, slightly, informing them of the Senator's latest financial state of affairs.

"The Senator has very little money. I am the one who

has financed all his business affairs. And I can assure you, gentlemen, that bank vault is closed. Everything you thought was the Senator's is mine. Every dime you thought he might have locked away, is mine."

Maria rose to her feet, and in an almost a whisper, she told them, "Gentlemen, this restaurant is closed, as of now."

Without waiting for a reply, she turned and strolled up onto the stage to stand in front of the microphone. Tapping the mouthpiece, she smiled and announced, "Ladies and Gentlemen. For those that do not know me, I am Maria Abbott, the Senator's wife."

As the applause started to break out, she held up her hands, saying, "No, No, Ladies and gentlemen, no applause, please. I am announcing that effective immediately, this facility is closed, and we are asking all of you to leave as quickly as possible."

Joseph, Lucas, and the three men seem to be mesmerized with Maria and failed to see the Senator walk up. They were not aware he was anywhere around until he asked, in an outraged tone, "Maria! What are you doing?"

The men may have been startled, but Maria showed no

sign of surprise as she turned, smiling sweetly at her husband. As she observed the quickly departing guests, she told him, "Well, Dear Husband, it appears that I have just shut down your little party. Oh, I would like for you to meet a couple of my friends. They are Liberty County Deputy Sheriff, Joseph Skywolf, and Lucas Wilson, our Governor's Special Investigator."

The blood drained from Abbott's face as he grabbed his wife's arm, only to find Joseph step between him and Maria, holding his right hand out toward the Senator, palm up. "Back off, Senator, and I won't put cuffs on you, Joseph told him."

Abbott collapsed in a nearby chair, trying to regain control of himself. Glaring at his wife, he tried to stay calm, as he asked, "What are you trying to do, get us both killed?"

"No. Well, maybe, just you," Maria said, with as much anger as she could muster.

Joseph was not waiting for Abbott to respond, and as he stepped to stand in front of the clearly-shaken man, he said, "Senator, we need to leave now!"

Looking from his wife to Joseph, with total confusion,

Abbott asked,

"Where are we going?"

Looking to Lucas for a suggestion, Joseph shrugged his shoulders and said,

"Figured, since your friends all left in a huff, we would give you a lift back to your jet. The flight back home might give you time to figure out what your next step is going to be."

Abbott stared at Joseph like a man processed, managing to squeak out, "Have you lost your mind?"

Lucas gave a snort, answering before Joseph could, "Naw, he hasn't, but I'm pretty sure I have." Lucas was tired of fooling with the Senator, so, he gave him the ultimatum,

"You come with us back to Texas. There's a State AG waiting to talk deal. You might live through all of this, or, you can find your own way back, and good luck."

Before Abbott could answer, Joseph added, "Get up and walk, now, we're leaving."

With these last words, Joseph, Lucas, and Maria Abbott turned and walked away. A scant ten seconds and the Senator was right with them. At the door, Joseph motioned for the others to wait while he stepped outside. Making sure the limousine they had taken from the airport was waiting for them, Joseph motioned for the driver to pull up. Once the limousine stopped in front of the restaurant, the driver jumped out, opening the driver's side door. Joseph opened the rear passenger side and motioned for the others to come out. Lucas took Maria's elbow and ushered her out and into the rear passenger seat, then went around and got into the driver's side. Joseph motioned for Abbott to follow. In what seemed to be only a split second, a black sedan, tires squealing, turned the corner heading straight at the limousine. Shoving Abbott into the limousine, Joseph yelled, "Down!" as he dropped down, pulling his gun. The windows on the passenger side of the sedan open and gunfire erupts. The whole incident took only seconds. Joseph had dropped down beside the limousine watched as the sedan turned at the next intersection and disappeared. Joseph jumped in beside Maria, who was in the rear seat, and yelled at the driver, "Get us out of here!"

The driver gunned the motor, squealed the tires, and drove away, asking in a scared voice, "Where to? Airport, or headquarters?"

Joseph answered, "Headquarters! This is Texas Senator Abbott. There's just been an attempt on his life."

The drive took less than ten minutes and three phone calls. One, from Lucas to the Governor, telling him about the shooting and to enable his help with the local cops. The second one to Jonathan, bringing him up to date, and the third, to Lillian, to let her know no one was hurt before the news media came alive with the reports of the attempt on the senator's life.

Sitting across the desk from the Vegas Chief of Police, Joseph and Lucas were quiet, as Chief Virgil Wilson dressed them down.

"You idiots come riding into my town like the Lone Ranger and engage in gunfire on the streets of my town. I should lock you up and throw away the key. Your bosses are going to hear about this."

Joseph chose his words carefully. He did not need for the chief to carry through on his threat.

"We were escorting Ms. Abbott, nothing more. Neither Lucas nor I returned fire, Chief Wilson."

"Great! That makes it all the better when I try and

explain how two hotshot law-guys came riding in our town uninvited and got into a shooting war with some of the local MS13 goons."

Glancing at Lucas who had suddenly sat up straighter in his chair, Joseph asked Wilson, "How do you know it was MS13 goons?"

"Because the ass butts didn't hit any of you, or anyone else. They can't shoot for spit." Wilson told them, trying hard not to split a gut, laughing.

Sobering a little, Wilson went on to tell them, "Besides your driver recognized one of the shooters. So, why would MS13 be shooting at you?"

"We are escorting the Senator back to Texas to face an inquiring by our AG. Senator Abbott is suspected of being involved with the Cartel."

Wilson released a soft whistle, but was shaking his head the next second, saying, "Don't get why our goons would care about Abbott."

"Because the MS13 is against the Cartel opening up a bigger operation here in Vegas, a bigger operation than what you already have," Lucas answered.

Leaning back in his chair, Wilson mulled around in his

head what Lucas had just told him. He did not like what hearing what he knew was the truth.

"So, what you're saying is that the Maria chain is controlled by the Cartel? Not just the new one here in Vegas, but in other parts of the country?"

Nodding, Joseph told him, "Yeah, and the one in Mexico, of course. Ms. Abbott is just learning about her husband's outside business and is taking steps to shut it down."

"If she lives long enough to do it, you mean," Wilson said, through gritted teeth.

Joseph nodded, having to agree. "Yeah, if we can keep her alive long enough."

Wilson stood, and, shaking his head, said, "If we can help, let us know. In the meantime, I think you should get your friends back to Texas."

Joseph and Lucas shook the chief's hand, thanked him, and followed him out to where the Abbotts were waiting.

"A couple of my guys will give you an escort to the air terminal," Wilson said. Looking at Abbott, he said, "Senator, you are not welcome back in my town, so I trust you will take that as a warning with regards to your safety."

Not waiting for a reply, Wilson turned and walked back to his office.

CHAPTER 12

By this time, they had boarded the plane, and it began its departure. Abbott was endeavoring to relax and to regain control of himself and of his situation. Moving over, he sat down in the seat next to his wife. Holding out his hand, he told her, "I need to use your phone."

Turning to face her husband, Maria removed her cell phone from her purse but hesitated to give it to him long enough to ask, "Why, why did you do this?"

For a moment, she thought he was not going to reply, but when he did, it was with a cruel, twisted smile. "I got fed up with being your husband, living off your father's money."

The words felt like a knife twisting in her stomach. Handing him her cell phone, she told him, "I hope you die," her voice, fierce.

Standing up, Abbott walked to the back of the plane to make his phone call. Joseph, who had been observing the exchange between the two, came over and sat down next to Maria, and asked, "You doing Okay?"

Nodding, Maria glanced back at her husband and said, "He

says it's my fault he got into bed with the drugs. My daddy's money, anyway."

Joseph grunted in disgust, "Yeah, sure, and I bet it's your daddy's money's fault he has lived the life of luxury all those years before the Cartel."

Smiling, Maria agreed. "I'm sure it would sound that way. What is our next step?"

"It depends on what your husband is cooking up as his next step." was his answer.

Maria was uncomfortable with the waiting and not knowing. "Do you think he will make a deal with the AG?"

"If he has any sense, he will." Looking back at Abbott, who was still on the phone, Joseph shook his head and answered her question. "Truth is, I doubt it. He's working on his slippery slope right now, and he is going to feel like he got a pass."

"They'll kill him." Maria asserted.

Joseph responded, "Most likely." With those last words, he walked away, seeing Abbott returning from the back. From the smirk on Abbott's face, Joseph was pretty sure that the Senator was not going to meet and talk with the Attorney General. The balance of the flight back to Texas was quiet, each with their own thoughts of what lay ahead. One thing Joseph knew for sure, he was picking up Lillian and taking her home. They had a wedding to plan.

A car and driver were waiting for the Senator, and without so much of a kiss-my-butt, he got in the vehicle and was out of sight within minutes. Lucas, Joseph, and Maria Abbott sat quietly in Jonathan's office, waiting until he finished his conversation with the Governor. Hanging up the phone, Jonathan could not help but feel sympathy for the three. Seeing their woebegone faces, it was evident how disappointed they were.

"Lucas, the Governor says he will have a word with you when you get back to the Capitol. He expects you back after delivering Ms. Abbott home," Jonathan said and turned to Joseph to say, "I really thought you had a little more sense than what you've shown. You all three could have been killed."

"Sheriff Lawrence, these boys went with me to protect me," Maria told Jonathan, breathlessly. "I should not have reacted so stupidly."

Jonathan wasn't appeased by her plea, and he let her know exactly how he felt. "You're right, you did not use good sense, and you could have gotten one or both killed, and I cannot afford to lose a good deputy."

"It won't happen again, Sheriff, I promise," Maria solemnly swore.

Joseph was quick to respond, "You're right, it won't. You are going home. Lucas is going to escort you and stay with you a few days. Until we see what direction your husband is going to jump, and what the AG is going to do next."

Looking at Joseph's face, Maria knew it would do her little good to argue the point. Besides, she wanted to go home; she needed to think.

Focusing his attention on Joseph, he told him, "I really did expect you to act differently, but it's done. Chester and I will escort Lucas and Ms. Abbott to their ride home. Lillian's waiting. I suggest you see what you can do to make sure she still intends to marry you."

A slight grin spread across Joseph's face as he stood. He shook hands with Lucas and said goodbye to Maria Abbott, then hurriedly left Jonathan's office before the sheriff could change his mind.

Joseph was not surprised at Lillian's reaction when he told her he was not sure she would be going home anytime soon. First of all, he was not sure her strength was totally recuperated, and he felt better that she was staying there with all the activities going on at the ranch. It was not likely anyone might try to harm her. Of course, the grocery store was also very active, and she had almost been killed there.

"The sheriff and his bride do not need me in their home! They are still Honeymooning!" Lillian knew she was too loud, but she was tired of Joseph not listening to her. She wanted to go home. She was not hiding anymore. Joseph also knew it would be useless to suggest she go home with him, so, reluctantly, he agreed to take her home.

"OK, but you have to promise you will not go bouncing all over town until the doctor totally dismisses you," he said.

A small smile spread across Lillian's face, as she told him, "I do not bounce."

"Yeah, I know," he said with a leer, and added, "You float like a sexy angel."

Less than an hour later, Lillian was walking through her home for the first time in what seemed like an eternity. She felt comfortable in her own shoes. Throwing her arms around Joseph, she gave out a small squeal, "I'm home!"

Joseph understood exactly how Lillian was feeling at the moment because that was exactly how he felt when he walked away from the university. But, he wanted Lillian to understand the danger to her was not yet over. Perhaps it was not as hot as before, but he wanted her to be careful and listen to him and Jonathan.

"Until we bring the Senator in, I want to have one of the deputies chauffeur you around, just to be on the safe side."

Opening her mouth to object, Lillian stopped. Studying Joseph's face, Lillian knew it would be a major job to change his mind on this, and she was very happy to be home to fight that battle.

"Do you really think Abbott thinks I'm a threat to him?" Lillian asked, a frown furrowing her brow.

"Until we know for sure, we will assume, yes," Joseph told her, adding, with a big grin, "I am not taking any chances with your beautiful neck."

Before Lillian could respond, Joseph's cell phone announced an incoming call which brought Sam, who had been curled up on Lillian's sofa, to an alert, sitting position. Lillian could tell by the changing expression on Joseph's face that the call did not bring good news. Hitting the off button, Joseph apologized to Lillian. "That was an officer assist call; I need to go."

Lillian managed an understanding smile and walked with him and Sam to the door. Kissing him on the cheek, she told him, "I have a big ham bone for Sam's dinner."

Glancing at Sam, whose ears had perked up at the sound of her name, Joseph said, "I'm leaving Sam to watch over you today." Grinning at her, he asked, "Are you going to have a ham bone for me, too?"

Giving him a small push, Lillian promised, "No I'll have a special dinner prepared, just for you."

After telling Sam to stay and watch after Lillian, Joseph all but skipped out to his car. Life was definitely looking better, and he was not about to let the coming day get to him, or so he thought.

Lillian and Sam stood in the doorway and watched Joseph drive away. Looking down at Sam, she smiled and said, "Come on girl, I'll see if I can find you that ham bone to chew on."

Arriving at the Liberty City Park, Joseph pulled up beside the parked, Deputy Sheriff's car. Chester walked up to meet him. Getting out of his car, the hairs on the nape of his neck stood up. Joseph knew his day had just landed in the outhouse.

"What's up, Chester?" he asked, with an effort in cordiality.

"Wasn't sure about that, so, I thought I'd better get you to take a look," Chester responded. Turning, he pointed to drops of red that lead them around and behind the brush lining the walking path. He stopped in front of what appeared to be a dead rat with its head chopped off. Then he pointed to a sheet of paper pinned to the rat's dead carcass with a six-inch nail.

Squatting down on his heels, Joseph read the crude writing. "The next dead rat could be you. BACK OFF." Straightening up, he told Chester, "Rope it off from the first drop of blood and get the CSI out here." Turning to go back to his car, he instructed Chester, "Stay with it until the lab crew wraps."

"What does it mean, Joseph?" Chester asked, not at all sure he was understanding anything that was happening.

"I don't know, Chester, but we are going to find out," Joseph answered him as he closed his car door and drove off, leaving Chester to wrap things up.

Turning on his cell phone speaker, Joseph pushed the number "4" and waited for an answer. On the second ring, Lucas greeted him with a cheery, "Hi, ho, Chief. What's up?"

"Just wondering what the Senator's been up to? Things are too quiet."

"Yeah, it is," Lucas said, adding, "However, the Senator's wife has been busy."

Joseph was not quite sure, but he would have almost sworn there was a note of skepticism in Lucas' voice.

"What do you mean, busy?" Joseph asked, with just the same twinge of skepticism on his part, as well.

"Well, the Lady gave a press release this morning, and the local TV people and the press covered it. Seems the Senator has had a nervous breakdown and will be resting at home. His Misses is stepping into his shoes, taking over the restaurant chain," Lucas told him, and added, "The Misses is taking a trip to Mexico to see if she will be closing the facility there."

"Oh, Hell!" was Joseph's short reply.

Lucas snort was not one of mirth, as he agreed with Joseph's sentiment, "Yeah, that's what I thought, too. The lady's going to get herself killed."

"What's the DEA saying about the Senator?"

"Quieter than a mouse; not one stinking word," Lucas spits out, adding, "The Governor ordered me to back off and let the DEA handle things, so I'm hamstrung."

"Well, I sure as hell ain't," Joseph said, through gritted teeth. Taking a deep breath, he asked, "How'd you like to take a vacation down Mexico way to see the Senator's lady?"

"Haven't had a vacation in a while......doesn't sound like a bad idea." Joseph told him, asking, "You tagging along?"

"Can't," Joseph grudgingly told him, "The Sheriff's still on his honeymoon, and we got an incident here I need to check out."

"Well, I guess I could just give the fair damsel a call and see if I can hitch a ride on her jet," Lucas told him, but he still was not happy about Joseph not going as well. "When is the sheriff due back?"

"Couple of days." Joseph isn't too happy about Lucas going it alone. "I wrap this rat killing thing up and I'll join you."

"Rat killing?" Lucas asked, with slight curiosity.

"Yeah, some joker killed a rat, chopped off its head, and pinned a note to its chest with a six-inch nail," Joseph said, adding, "Note said to back off."

"Back off what?' Lucas questioned, with a touch of uneasiness.

Joseph tone of voice gave evidence of his exasperation.

"Yeah, that's a good question, and that is what I am going to try to figure out."

"Well," Lucas conjured up, "maybe the warning was meant for the rat's friends."

"Ha, ha, very funny," came as a snarl from Joseph's lips.

Recognizing that Joseph had lost all sense of humor on the subject of the rat killing, Lucas changed it, quickly. "It doesn't seem strange to you that Mrs. Abbott, after all her posturing against her husband, has taken him back into the bosom of her home?"

"Yea, it seems odd but, there's not a hell of a lot I can do about it right now." Joseph countered.

"Well, I'll keep you posted. Hope the lady knows what she's doing," was Lucas' caustic reply.

Hanging up, Joseph had the same, silent thought. The buzz on his intercom and Lillian's replacement on the front desk, Nancy J, announced, "Joseph, there's a DEA agent here to see you."

Standing Joseph told her, "Send him in." More than one runaway train of thought was speeding through Joseph's head, as the tall, muscular, dark-haired agent walked in. Joseph's last runaway thought was, "Oh hell," as he walked around the desk, hand out, stretched to greet his next nightmare.

"If I'd known it was you, I'd told Nancy to tell you to get

lost." He said, his greeting convivial.

Shaking Joseph's hand, John Griffith's smile was whole-hearted as he returned the warm greeting. "When my boss told me I had to come here, I almost resigned. How are you, you old renegade?"

"Doing good, until you walked in," Joseph answered.

Sitting down across from Joseph's desk, Griffith shook his head and informed Joseph why he was there.

"It has come to our attention that you have a fellow we have some interest in, stashed away somewhere safe on the QT."

Sitting back in his chair, Joseph felt the hairs of forewarning on the nape of his neck, rising, "That fellow's name wouldn't be McCain, would it?" he asked, with just a touch of admonition.

"Yeah, it would be," Griffith said, adding, "I need to talk with McCain."

The old saying about the stone-faced Indian expression proved true with the sudden shut-down of Joseph's face, and the sudden coldness of the tone of his voice gave warning to tread carefully.

"Talk with? Sounds like you want to have a beer with a buddy. Is that what McCain is now, a buddy of the DEA?"

If Griffith had given any thought to how he should approach Joseph with the subject of McCain he would have first of all realized it was not going to be an easy walk in the park. Griffith had read the report on what had happened to Lillian, and what Joseph had done to bring McCain in. He had also read the speculation on the relationship between Lillian and Joseph, so, he knew it had taken a tremendous amount of willpower for Joseph to bring McCain in alive. It would take a tremendous amount of persuasion to talk him into letting McCain go.

Griffith started to explain, "He's not our buddy but...,"

Joseph interrupted him, saying, "And there is always a but, with the DEA, right?"

"Not exactly." Griffith tried to keep his answer friendly. He and Joseph had crossed swords before, and things could get ugly, but he needed Joseph right now. "McCain has information we need on a cartel gang called Los Triads Diazos."

"The Three Devils? That's a new one, isn't it?" Joseph was not sure Griffith was being upfront or not, but he definitely had him interested.

"Yeah, that's why we want to talk to McCain. He has been tied back to the three, and I want to know who, why, and how. When these guys come after you, they don't just come after you; they come after your entire family."

Getting to his feet Joseph was not happy about revealing McCain's whereabouts, but he appreciated Griffith's position. "He's in Huntsville. I'm going with you," he informed Griffith.

The drive to the Huntsville State penitentiary took two

hours, but having to park, going through security, and being ushered into the secure visiting room where McCain would be brought, took almost another hour. The drive time, and getting to see McCain, gave Joseph time to think. He was not so sure he liked what kept pressing to the front of his thoughts. If Abbott wasn't the main cog in the illegal dope ring here in the states, the possibilities were staggering.

Joseph was broken from his thoughts as McCain was ushered in. Joseph quickly acquired a new worry as he studied McCain's gaunt face. "Are you being fed enough?" he asked before he really gave it much thought. McCain gave him a brief smile of appreciation and assured him, "Yeah, just been having some stomach problems."

Walking over to a small round table, Joseph motioned for McCain to sit down. He and Griffith sat down facing him. Griffith came straight to the point of the meeting and asked, "What do you know about the Los Triads Diazos bunch?"

McCain looked from Joseph to Griffith, questioning, "Who the hell is this?"

Trying not to smirk, Joseph introduced the two men. "This is DEA Special Agent John Griffith; you can answer his questions."

McCain leaned back in his chair and, shaking his head, said, "What I know about that bunch is enough to get me and you both killed. What I don't know could get me and you both skinned alive and stacked out on an ant hill."

Griffith tried not to show his excitement at McCain's statement, but this was the huge glimmer of hope he had not expected.

"Would some of this knowledge be who their ties are to the US members in the Mexican drug hierarchy?" Griffith asked, with just a tad of hopefulness.

McCain remained silent a few seconds longer than what seemed normal. He studied Griffith, before answering, "Now that is what could get not only my throat cut but yours and all our family's throats cut. So, before I say another word, I want a deal, one better than the one this Indian cop gave me."

The idea that McCain could walk after hurting Lillian was one that Joseph had trouble keeping silent on.

"You're not walking out of here, so what are you asking for?" Griffith asked before Joseph could speak.

McCain nodded, acknowledging that he understood that he would not walk, but he had demands, and he made them known. "Like I said, I tell you what you want to know I put my life out there." Looking at Joseph, he added, "I've done some things I have to answer for, but not my family." Turning back to Griffith, he continued, "My wife, Jessica, lives in Oklahoma City with my ten-year-old son, Bryon, and her mother. I want them picked up, given a new identity, relocated, and my wife given financial help and a career of her choosing."

Joseph and Griffith were silent, digesting what McCain had just told them, but before either could speak, McCain made his last demand. "I don't want anyone but the Indian and his Australian cohort to handle the new identification and relocation. I don't know how you plan on doing it, nor do I care, but those are my demands. Once they are carried, out I'll give you the information you want."

Standing, McCain handed a piece of paper to Joseph and gave one last piece of advice. "If I were you, I'd keep this conversation between you two and the Aussie. Only someone you trust would stand between you and a bullet." Now waiting for either man to reply, McCain walked out without looking back.

Both men sat in silence, going over the implications and the demands that McCain had left them with. Joseph was the first one to speak, and it wasn't something Griffith wanted to hear.

"You have a mole in your department," Joseph announced, with a slight connotation as he unfolds the piece of paper McCain had given him. The name, Wendy McCain, and an address in Oklahoma City were written on it.

"Yeah," Griffith said, drawing the word out. Knowing the effect this new information could have on his investigation, he was not sure just what to say. "There are only one or two who that might be. It'll take me a little time to ferret the rat out. In the meantime, you have a chore ahead; think you can do what McCain asked without the US Marshall's help?"

"All I need is Jonathan and Lucas, and a whole lot of luck," Joseph declared, with more assurance than he felt.

Arriving back at his office, the first thing he had to do was call Lucas. It was not until Lucas answered with a cocky, "Howdy partner," that he was able to take a deep breath.

"You on your way to Mexico yet?" he asked crossing his fingers.

Lucas gave a disgusted snort, and told him, "Naw. The lady postponed the trip a couple of days. Seems the Senator ain't feeling so hot."

"Great, I need you back here asap," Joseph informs him.

"What's up?" Lucas asked, but had a gut feeling he wasn't about to find out, not yet anyway. He was getting to the point of knowing Joseph pretty good, and if he wasn't wrong, he knew Joseph would wait to tell him the pertinent facts in person. He wasn't proven wrong, as Joseph told him, "We'll talk in the morning when you get here; in the meantime, watch your back."

Hanging up his telephone, Lucas felt a shiver run up his back. "Oh hell," he thought, he didn't need the built-in alarm system he had been blessed with since birth, showing back up.

Where the hell was it when he was almost killed a few weeks ago? He had really thought that jinx was long gone. It seemed he was not going to be that blessed. What was that old saying his nanny had taught him, "once blessed twice cursed." It certainly was beginning to look like the twice-cursed hex was showing up.

CHAPTER 13

McCain's wife was not what Joseph expected. Jessica McCain was twenty-eight-years-old, which meant she gave birth when she was eighteen. Soft brown hair, with bright blue eyes that seem to sparkle, and a trim, shapely figure. The ten-year-old boy, Bryon, was the image of his mother, well-mannered and well disciplined. The mother, Ellen Bishop, was a typical Jewish mother who did not suffer fools easily, and one that would put a bullet through your heart just as easily as she would a knife. Jessica McCain had a furious guard dog but her mother would stand little chance from the scum that would come after McCain's family.

Sitting across the small breakfast table from Jessica McCain in Ellen Bishop's house, Joseph tried once more to make McCain's wife understand why she had to rip up her and her son and mother's life by the roots and move to another part of the world; why they had to change their identity. He was thankful Lucas had taken the boy outside, for what he was about to tell his mother, the boy did not need to hear.

"Ms. McCain, your husband sent me here to take you to a place where you, your son, and your mother will be safe." Joseph paused just long enough to take a deep breath, before continuing. "He has enemies that will come for you, your son, and your mother and your deaths would be agony. Do you understand that these enemies of your husband would not just kill you, they would crucify you? It would not matter that your son is only ten years old. It would not matter that your mother is seventy years old."

Jessica was noticeably shaken this time, but her reluctance to leave her home and any chance of seeing or being with her husband was still evident as she made another plea, "If I do what you say, leave everything and everyone that I care about, I take my son and mother and move across the world to Australia, what about my husband?"

"Your husband is going to spend the rest of his life in some brick cell, under protective custody." Joseph knew he was being harsh, but he wanted the woman to understand the life she knew was no more. "He will die there; you just need to choose how and where you want to die."

Jessica was struggling not to cry, and in the process, was making Joseph feel even worse. "Ms. McCain, you're young, and you have a great son. You can build a new and happier life, and it's what your husband wants."

Ellen Bishop, the girl's mother had sat quietly, making no comment and listening intently, interrupted before her daughter could speak. "I have always known what kind of a man Thomas McCain is, and when he married Jessie, she was only seventeen, she was pregnant. He promised me that he would take care of Jessie and raise my grandson as his. He has never disappointed me. He has kept his word. How he made his living has never touched us, not until now."

Looking at her daughter, she fought back tears as she pleaded, "If Thomas wants this for you, then it is what you should do. He is still trying to protect you and Bryon. He loves that boy and you, and perhaps you two are the only love he has ever known. Let him do this."

Jessica closed her eyes, taking a slow, deep breath. It was several moments before she spoke. "If my husband wants me to do this, I will, but I want to see him before anything takes place."

Joseph opened his mouth to say he did not think that was such a good idea, but just as quickly closed it, without speaking. Seeing the determined look on Jessica's face, he said, "I'll arrange it but. You are to pack up; you, your son, and your mother, right now. Take only the clothes you will need for two days. We are leaving here today, and Jessica McCain, her son, and her mother will vanish." Seeing that both women were about to object, he added, "That is not negotiable. You do the packing, or I will."

Joseph was sure that both women were going to refuse, but was pleasantly surprised when they both rose and said, softly, "Very well."

Taking a deep breath, he released it in one big puff. He really hated dealing with women who were trying to deal with grief. He was sure it most likely had something to do with him being a 'heap big redskin.' At least that's what Jonathan would have said. Going outside, he found Lucas and the boy sitting on the porch swing. Seeing Joseph come out, Lucas got up and walked over to join him, but the boy chose that moment to go into the house to find his mother.

"What's our next step?" Lucas questioned.

"They're packing, and we are taking them back with us. We will put them in a hotel room where they will be instructed on their new identities." Glancing back toward the front door, Joseph half expected the McCain woman to come out to announce she had changed her mind. It had all been too easy. With some concern for speed, he asked Lucas, "How soon can you have everything ready?"

"Forty-eight hours. I can have passports, IDs, and a new residence ready." Lucas assured him, adding, "I will be the only person living who will know who she becomes and where she will be living. I will not even tell you." Lucas paused a moment before asking, "And what are her demands?"

Releasing a small sigh, Joseph told him, "She wants to see her husband."

"Oh hell," was the instant response from Lucas, before he asked, "Can you arrange it without getting us all killed?"

A slight smirk twisted Joseph's lips, as he said, 'I sure as hell plan on it.

Joseph was not happy about the arranged meeting between McCain and his wife, but like it or not, it was taking place. Waiting in the warden's office, which Warden Phillip Winters had reluctantly agreed to vacate for the McCain reunion, Joseph hoped he had not made a big mistake. Glancing at the nervously twitching McCain woman, he was beginning to get that familiar twinge up his spin he got when things were about to go wrong.

The sudden opening of the door startled both Joseph and Jessica, who rose to their feet as Warden Pete Cushings walked in, looking extremely agitated. Cushings looked from Jessica to Joseph, and finally managed to say, "Deputy, I need to talk to you." Before Joseph could reply, Cushings turned and escaped back out the door.

Following the warden out into the hall, Joseph waited for him to speak.

"McCain is being taken to the hospital in Huntsville," Cushings announced, on a breathless note.

For some reason, Joseph felt no surprise at the news. It had always been a foregone conclusion that sooner or later McCain was going to be silenced, so, Joseph's calm question of "What happened?" seemed perfectly normal.

"Our doctor is not sure. McCain's unconscious." Shaking his head, the Warden added, "He thinks it's some kind of poison, he's just not sure. We had him isolated. He was watched 24/7, no one got near him."

"I suggest you start checking out those who were watching McCain," Joseph said, with a touch of venom. "You have a traitor amongst your staff."

Joseph whirled and went back to the warden's office to face McCain's wife. Jessica McCain knew something was wrong, from Joseph's expression. She rose to her feet upon his entrance, and asked, "What's happened to my husband?"

"We are not sure, Ms. McCain. He is on his way to the Huntsville hospital right now…"

"Take me there!" she demanded, interrupting Joseph. The demand came as no surprise; Joseph expected no less. Turning, he opened the door for Jessica, saying softly, "Yes ma'am."

The drive to the hospital took half an hour. It was done in total silence. Joseph was thankful for his sirens. The news that awaited them at the hospital was again expected by Joseph but came as a hard blow to Jessica. She was sitting quietly on a chair against the wall in the emergency waiting room, still stunned at the sudden news about her husband. Joseph kept an eye on her while he stood and talked with the doctor.

"McCain was under security, what happened?" was the one question Joseph wanted to be answered. The doctor's answer was brief. "Rat poisoning." Now the burning question that Joseph wanted to be answered, became, "How did he get rat poisoning."

Dialing the warden's number, Joseph was blunt when the warden answered. "Place the guards who were responsible for McCain's safety under arrest. One of them poisoned McCain."

The warden's, "We're on that now," was all Joseph needed. Next, he dialed Lucas, who was waiting back at the sheriff's office. When Lucas answered, he told him, "Put a deputy back out at Lillian's."

"You think they'll go after her again? "Lucas questioned.

"It looks like they may try clearing up some loose ends, and Lillian is one of them." Joseph answered, adding, "Lillian is gonna split a gut, so, tell Chester to stand pat."

Lucas gave a soft chuckle and said, "I sure do not envy him that task."

Hanging up, Joseph walked over to Jessica. "Ms. McCain, you and I need to talk; lets' go have a cup of coffee. The doctor will keep us posted on your husband."

Standing, Jessica took a deep breath and seem to change from a young immature girl to a strong mature woman, as she quietly informed Joseph,

"Deputy Skywolf, my husband is dying and I want to be with him when he does. Take me to him now, please."

Hesitating for only a brief moment, Joseph nodded, turned and lead her down the hall to the ICU door. Stopping in front of the door, he stepped back, allowing Jessica to enter, then closed it with a hard, cold expression on his face as Jessica entered.

Half an hour later, Jessica came out of the ICU, her eyes red and puffy, and Joseph knew she had been crying. Squaring her shoulders as though ready for a battle, Jessica told him, "He's gone."

Joseph hated being the bad guy, but, with McCain dead, he had to make some major changes in any cohesive plans he had conjured up. "I am sorry for your loss, Ms.

McCain, but we need to leave now."

Once again, Jessica McCain summoned an inner strength, as she informed Joseph, "I will not leave here until final arrangements are made for my husband."

"Ms. McCain...." Whatever Joseph had been about to say, Jessica cut him short.

"My husband is not to be buried in the penitentiary cemetery. He is to be cremated and my son and I will scatter his ashes." Taking a deep breath, she added quickly, before Joseph could make any reply, "This is not negotiable."

Realizing it would do little good to argue with her, Joseph unclipped his phone, pushed in Lucas' number again, and when he answered, told Lucas,

"Cancel travel plans for Ms. McCain. Take her family and check them into a hotel. Then meet me back at the sheriff's office."

The drive to the courthouse was done in silence. Lucas was waiting in the parking lot. He got out of his truck and walked over to Joseph, grinning.

"Thought I'd give you a heads up. Lillian's waiting in the dispatcher's office, and she ain't happy, Mate," he told

Joseph, doing little to suppress his glee.

Joseph muttered a soft, "hell," and told Lucas, "Take Ms. McCain to the Sheriff's office. I'll meet you there."

Lucas gave a smart salute, and still grinning, turned to Jessica. "Ms. McCain, let's you and I go into Sheriffs Lawrence's office. Joseph will be joining us there."

Joseph did not wait to see Lucas take charge of Jessica, but with long strides, headed for the Dispatcher's office. Lillian was waiting, and her folded arms resting across her breast gave proof she was indeed an unhappy camper. Not waiting for Joseph to speak first, she demanded, "And when were you going to tell me about your visit to the penitentiary?"

"I was going to call you…" Joseph started to explain, only to be cut short by Lillian, who realizes she is acting like some crazy fish wife. She threw her arms around him and said, "I'm sorry, I'm sorry, I'm sorry."

Holding her close, Joseph planted a quick kiss on her lips, and apologized as well, "I should have called you; forgive me?" That said, he stepped back, and asked, "You get any phone calls from anyone asking you questions about what you know about McCain?"

Shaking her head, Lillian's answer was slow in coming. "Yeah, a Judge Leroy Preston. He said he was part of a task force the Governor's put together."

Anticipating the worse, Joseph held his breath, as questioned, "What did you tell him?"

Grinning, Lillian replied, "I ain't no cotton picker from the deep South, honey. I

told him I didn't know nothing. Really sorry I couldn't help him."

Despite his concern, Joseph had to laugh at Lillian's pitiful drawl. "Woman, you just insulted a bunch of hot-blooded Southerners."

"You forget, honey, I'm black, I can get away with it," Lillian informed him, with a smile.

Joseph was not sure Lillian was right about her assumption, but he let her win that one, as he told her, "McCain's dead. We have his wife, mother-in-law, and his son in protective custody."

The light-hearted banter was gone, as Lillian was clearly shocked. "Dead! How?"

Joseph quickly brought Lillian up to date, finally telling her, "Ms. McCain is in Jonathan's office with Lucas waiting for me. Her son and mother are at the hotel. We have two deputies outside of their door."

Clearly, this is not what Lillian wanted to hear. "What are you going to do?"

Shaking his head, Joseph gave her a crooked smile. "I do not have the slightest idea, but I am about to find out."

Taking a deep breath, he told Lillian, "Get ahold of the Protective Witness Services and tell them we have one for them. They need to take Ms. McCain, her son, and mother, today." Before Lillian could voice an opinion, he asked her, "Would you want to join us after the call?"

"You have to ask?" was Lillian's answer, as she turned and walked quickly toward her desk to call the US Marshall offices."

Smiling for a brief moment, Joseph turned and walked toward the sheriff's office door. He is pretty sure, right at that moment, that he could now understand how a prisoner might feel walking down the hall to the door to the execution room.

Joseph was feeling the old familiar trigger crawling up his spin. Seated across from Jessica McCain, he knew the other shoe was about to drop. Reaching into the tote bag she had insisted on carrying, she removed a small brown notebook. Handing it to Joseph she told him, "Last year my husband gave me this notebook and asked that I keep it for him. If anything were to happen to him, I was not to read it, but pass it on to someone I trusted."

Taking the notebook, Joseph began flipping the pages, scanning them as Jessica continued, "I know what my husband did for a living. I also know how he treated me, my son and my mother. I want him avenged but most of all I want my son to know that he redeemed himself in the eyes of the Lord and that he was a good man at the end."

Joseph certainly did not agree with Jessica's assessment of John McCain, but the pages of McCain's notebook kept him from expressing his thoughts on the subject of McCain's repentance.

Handing the notebook to Lucas, he instructed, "Give this to Lillian and have her make 2 copies of every page. Then get ahold of the Governor and set up a meeting for tomorrow morning with him and the heads of our state law officials. Make sure it's with those he can trust."

Waiting until Lucas is out of the office, Joseph turned back to Jessica McCain, letting her know what the next step would be, as far as she was concerned.

"A Marshall from the Federal Protective Services will be here this afternoon. They will take you and your family to a secure place, and you will start learning your new identification." Anticipating an objection, Joseph continued, quickly,

"You understand, none of this is debatable. You will be removed from my custody today. When your husband's ashes are ready, I will notify the US Marshall's service and they will handle it from there. Once the ashes are dispensed, you will be relocated, and you and I will have no further contact. It is for you and your family's safety."

A knock on the office door stopped further conversation, as Lucas stuck his head in and announced, "The Marshall is here for Ms. McCain."

Standing, Joseph walked around the desk to stand in front of Jessica. Hesitating for only a moment, Jessica rose and took his hand in a firm grip, telling him,

"Deputy, thank you. Know that I am depending on you to see that due justice is handed down on all those involved in my husband's death."

The office door was opened wider as Lucas ushered the

Marshall in, and the care, the protection, and the security for Jessica McCain and her family are finally lifted from Joseph's shoulders. As Jessica and the Marshall walked out, Lillian entered with the small notebook and a stack of papers in her hands, with Sam following. Handing the notebook and papers to Joseph, she said,

"There were only five pages, but from what I read, that's more than enough." Looking down at Sam who sat patiently waiting for her next move, she added. "And, you do not leave this sweet shadow with me when you leave." Seeing the beginnings of a smile on Joseph's face, she shakes her finger in his face. "I can't even go to the bathroom without her sticking to me like glue. You are taking her with you." Without choking on her own laughter, she stormed out of the room with Sam hot on her heels.

Making a sudden stop, Lillian turned back to Joseph, barely avoiding stumbling over Sam, and walked back over to stand in front of Joseph. Her concern for Joseph's safety was chewing away at her, and she knew she would have little to say, or do when it came to him not taking whatever next steps he would be taking. Before she could say anything, Joseph stepped up closer, just inches from her, and in a soft, low voice, told her, "I will not take any unnecessary chances, and I will have my back covered at all times. Love you, but I have to do this."

Sighing, Lillian's answer was one of surrender. "I know you do." Leaning forward, she gave him a swift kiss on the lips, then told him, "But, I promise, if you get killed, I will stack you out on an ant hill," and walked out of the office, giving Lucas a big smile as she walked past him.

Lucas, who was an uncomfortable witness to the exchange between Joseph and Lillian, caught her smile and almost choked on a snort of laughter. With his eyes cutting daggers at Lucas, Joseph went back and sat down behind Jonathan's desk, picked up one of the copies Lillian had given him, and handed it to Joseph, telling him, "Be prepared to be stunned."

It took Lucas only a few moments to read the condensed page. When he finished, he laid it down on a knee, and in a voice as cold as ice, says, "She played us for a couple of jackasses."

"Well," Joseph said, not sure the word jackass was a strong enough adjective, but the only other one he could think of was "a couple of dumbasses," for sure.

"The Governor sent a text a few minutes ago. A chopper will pick us up to join him and a company of Rangers at his ranch in Breckenridge. He wants everything; raids, arrest, and what all, synched," Lucas answered, adding, "Told him the Senator and wife were ours. He agreed."

"Good," was Joseph's only reply. The thought of Maria Abbott's deception was an itch Joseph needed to ease, and putting the handcuffs on her would be the only way.

"Is the chopper here?" Joseph asked as he stood and walked around the desk. Lucas nodded, a grim look on his face as he answered, "Yeah." As far as Joseph was concerned, that said it all.

CHAPTER 14

Sitting in the Governor's war room, Joseph scanned the room carefully. There were five Texas Rangers present, along with General Pete Mullins. Standing with Lucas, he was able to access the five Rangers and felt comfortable with them, but Mullins he was still having a problem with. Turning to speak to Lucas, he was interrupted by the Governor and his assistant who were entering the room.

The Governor greeted the gathered men with, "Gentlemen, take a seat." He sat down behind his desk. His face was stern.

"To start things off, I want to introduce to those of you who do not know them, Special Investigator for the Governor's office, Lucas Wilson and Deputy Sheriff Joseph Skywolf."

Nodding toward his assistant, he continued, "My assistant, Sylva Perry, is passing out special warrants for State Senator Abbott and his wife Maria, and State Justice, Rayburn Stevenson. Looking at Joseph, the Governor gave a small smile, saying, "I understand you and Lucas want the honors with the Senator and his wife?"

Both Joseph and Lucas answered with a firm, "Yes Sir!"

"Very well. You will take three Rangers with you." He looked toward a tall, masculine Ranger sitting back against the wall, and introduced him, "Captain William Henry Thomas. He will be making the actual arrest. You will have two Rangers as your escort"

Seeing that the two were about to object, he said, "Joseph, you are out of your jurisdiction, and Lucas, you are a special investigator out of the Governor's office. I want these arrests above board and unquestionable. Understood?"

Not liking it, both Joseph and Lucas, never-the-less, nodded "yes."

Relieved that the two men were not going to make a fuss, the Governor continued. "The remaining two Rangers, Sargent Zeke Daniels, and Ranger Ed Franks will pick up Justice Stevenson. I asked General Mullins here so he can be prepared to be a spokesperson for my office. The moment handcuffs are placed, he will be talking to the news people."

Feeling the vibration of his cell phone, Joseph removed it, glanced at the calling party name, and got up and quickly left the room. Outside in the hall, he answered, "Skywolf."

Lillian, who was on the other end, told him, "They've arrested the man who poisoned McCain." Before Joseph could ask, she told him, "It was one of the guards, just as expected."

"And you called to tell me this because?" was Joseph's response.

"The guy wants to talk to you. Says he won't talk to anyone but you, the only one he trusts."

Joseph's groan was quite audible. "Hell, he better have something worth saying, or I'm gonna gut shoot him."

Startled, Lillian warns, 'Hush, you can't say things like that on an open line."

Smiling, despite how he was feeling at the moment, Joseph snorted, saying, 'Well, I just did. Has Chester found out anything more about the dead varmint?"

Lillian let his question slide, and answered, "No, not yet. Most likely won't be anything other than some school kid trying to be cool."

"Yeah," Joseph said, adding, "most likely. Alright, tell the Warden I'll be there in an hour."

Shutting the cell down, Lucas and the two Rangers walk out as he tells him the latest happening. Shaking his head, Lucas did not sound the least bit disappointed that Joseph is not going to be in on the taking down of the Abbotts.

"Sorry Mate, I'll be sure and give Ms. Abbott your best wishes," Lucas said, grinning from ear to ear.

"Yeah, I just bet you are," was Joseph's reply. Glancing down at Sam, who had been sitting quietly beside him, he reached down and scratched the top of her head. Looking back at Lucas, he said, "Take Sam with you; she can use some fun time."

Grinning, Lucas spoke to Sam. "Hey Mate, want to go with me?" The excitement in Sam is clearly seen as she hears the word "go."

As Joseph glared at Lucas, it was also evident that he is mentally planning the wrath he will dump on the warden.

Landing the Ranger's chopper on the front lawn of the

Abbott house, Lucas jumped out, with Sam hot on his heels. His sharp, "Sam," brought her to attention. Doing a semicircle swing with his left arm, he said, "Recon!" With the command, Sam was off at a trot.

To say Lucas was surprised when the front door of Maria Abbott's home was opened by the lady herself, would be a true statement. Smiling, she stepped back, welcoming Lucas and the two Rangers.

"Gentlemen, come in. I have been expecting you." Not waiting for an answer, Maria turned and walked back into her sitting room where she sat down on a small sofa and motioned for the men to sit, as well.

"Please, be seated. I would like to offer you a cup of coffee or tea, but I am afraid there is no staff help. I let them all go home," she said, with a small smile.

"Ms. Abbott, where is your husband?" Lucas asked, with a growing knowledge that things were not right with Maria Abbott. She answered, "The Senator had some friends pick him up.... just a few...moments before...you arrived." Lucas knew he was right, but he asked anyway. "Ms. Abbott, are you alright?"

If Maria heard or even understood the question, she

paid no mind to it, as she gave a small smile, saying, "The Senator…. was foolish to…. go with …. those…. men. I …. chose to stay." Taking a deep breath, she seemed to sit up straighter and taller, saying, with a more forceful tone, "You gentlemen must leave now…I am very sleepy…."

Looking at the two Rangers who had been standing by, watching the exchange, Lucas' voice raised, as he ordered. "Rev up the chopper; we're taking her to the closest hospital."

Shaking her head Maria, slowly told him, "My dear boy…its…much too…late for…that." With her last words, Maria's head slumped onto her chest. Leaning over her, Lucas checked for a pulse in her neck, and a soft, "Damn," told the results.

Stepping back, Lucas removed his cell phone from his belt, punched the Governor's number, and when the call was answered, he said, "We need a CSI team out at Maria Abbott's ranch, and a fugitive warrant issued on the Senator."

The Governor's reply of, "Hell!" and the sound of the dial tone completed Lucas' day as one of a really crappy one.

Hearing frantic barking from outside, Lucas told the Rangers, "Go through the house to be sure there is no one else here." Not waiting for a response, Lucas made a quick dash for the door, knowing Sam did not break silence unless there was a pressing danger.

Waiting just outside the door, Sam turned, making a dead run for the tree lines off to the west, with Lucas hot on her trail. Twenty yards in, Sam came to a halt, and it was only a few seconds later that Lucas, too, stops. Standing next to Sam, he followed her gaze, upward.

Senator John Abbott's body was hanging from a tall pine, like a pieta; the body had been impaled on it. A pool of blood had puddled directly beneath the body. It was obvious that Abbott had been pushed or thrown from the helicopter that he had been picked up in, just minutes before.

Removing his cell phone, Lucas pushed the Governor's number again. When he answered, Lucas told him, "You need to prepare a press release. Abbott is dead."

The Governor gave a short, "How?" Lucas did not need to hear the curse words the Governor had released before the harsh "how," to know that things, indeed, were in the old handbasket of hell.

"Looks like his friends were fed up with taking care of their Senator. Figure they pushed him out the chopper to see if he could fly," Lucas told him.

Joseph walked into warden's office where Cushings was waiting. Standing, the warden held out his hand, greeting him with, "I would never have suspected any of my guards, least of all, Frank Kingston."

Understanding was not something Joseph was willing to give the warden right then, but he went light on him. "Where is Kingston now?" he asked.

"I have Texas Ranger, Jefferson Davis, in an outer office holding Kingston down the hall. I wanted him kept away from the other personnel."

It was not easy not commenting on the ranger's name, but Joseph figured the warden had heard all such comments before, so he nodded and agreed that the warden had done the right thing in isolating Kingston. "Thanks, that was good thinking. Can you have him brought in?"

Pushing the intercom on his desk, Cushings snapped, "Have Kingston brought in." Standing, he walked to the door and opened it for the ranger and Kingston to enter.

"Take a seat, Kingston," he said. "This is Deputy Sheriff Joseph Skywolf."

With the introductions done, Cushings and the Ranger exit, leaving Joseph and Kingston alone.

Kingston did not wait for Joseph to start the conversation, as he burst out, "You have to make sure I don't get sent to any facility in Texas. We have to agree on that before I tell you anything."

Studying the guard, Joseph knew the guy was scared, and from everything he had begun to find out about the Abbotts and their circle, the guy had a right to be scared.

"You give me something I can find proof on, and I will see what I can do," was his promise to Kingston.

Taking a moment to decide if he could live with Joseph's offer, and deciding that most likely that was all that was going to be offered, Kingston nodded and started telling what he knew.

"I was approached by a representative of Senator Abbott's and offered twenty thousand dollars to take care of McCain." Knowing how bad what he had just said sounded, Kingston hurriedly added, "You have to understand. I was losing my house, and my family was going to be kicked out onto the streets."

"So, you sold your soul for thirty pieces of silver?" was Joseph's reply. "Abbott's dead. You don't have a lot to offer, do you?"

The stunned expression on Kingston's face told Joseph that the man did not have any knowledge of what happened to Abbott.

"So, who was the associate of Abbott's that paid you the visit?" Joseph asked, more or less bracing him for the next shock, and it was, indeed, one he had not expected.

"Said he was some retired general; a personal friend of the Governor's, so, I should trust him to do what was best for me."

Stunned, Joseph sat without speaking for several moments. Then he rose to his feet, walked over to the door, opened it, and motioned for the Texas Ranger to come in.

Looking at Kingston, he spoke in harsh tones. "You are going to be taken to a deep, dark hideaway. You will have no contact with anyone for the next forty-eight hours."

Stepping closer, he asked, "Do you understand what I am saying? If you want to save your hide, you will do exactly what I say, understood?"

Kingston nodded, too stunned, at the moment, to speak. Satisfied that the guard understood, Joseph turned back to the Ranger.

"Deliver this guy to Liberty County jail. There's a deputy there named Chester. You and Chester are not to leave this man; not even for toilet breaks." Joseph was sure the Ranger understood, but to add icing to the cake, he added, "Your life, your job, everything you hold dear, is on the line here. Keep this guy alive."

Nodding, the Ranger assured him, "Yes, Sir, I understand." Walking over to Kingston, he told him to turn around. He handcuffed him and lead him out of the office. Watching them leave, Joseph took his cell phone from his belt, pushed in Lucas' number, and when the Aussie answered, he asked, "Just how much do you trust our Governor?"

If Lucas was surprised by the question, he gave no indication, answering, "With my life. Why?"

"Because that's where our leak is coming from," Joseph told him, with little joy.

"Hell no!" Lucas is stunned now. "No way; the Governor is one that is beyond reliable. He is not mixed up in any drug money."

"We need to talk to him. How do we manage it without giving it away to anyone?"

Lucas was silent for a few seconds, before saying, "We walk right in through the Capital's front doors, sit down and have a cup of Joe, and ask him if he's an upstanding gent or Hyena bait."

"And you think you can tell the difference between lie or truth?" Joseph asked.

"Yeah," Lucas said. "I will be able to tell the difference."

Taking a deep breath, Joseph pushed the last gnawing bit of doubt away. "Okay, wrap up the mess there, and I will meet you at the Capital's front door." Glancing at his cell phone, he continued, "at three o'clock."

"Man, that's just forty-five minutes from now!" was Lucas' response, after checking his phone as well.

"Means you need to get a move on," Joseph told him, and pushed the disconnect button.

The flight to Austin would take him at least half an hour. Joseph pushed Jonathan's telephone number. He had fifteen minutes to convince the Sheriff he had not lost his mind.

Explaining to Jonathan was easier than what Joseph had expected. Wrapping things up, he told Jonathan, "Lucas and I are going to talk to the Governor in about half an hour. Lucas wants to face him with what we know, and see his reaction."

"You trust Lucas to be able to read a guy who has spent half his life lying to the voters of this state?" was Jonathan's one and only question.

Joseph was aware that he had not known Lucas for very long, but in the time that he has known him, the Aussie had saved his butt more than once, so, he owed him at least this one.

"Yeah, I think he can handle it," was his answer.

"Alright, then get going," Jonathan told him, hanging up.

CHAPTER 15

Lucas was waiting for Jonathan on the front steps of the state capital, and he did not look happy, as he said, "The Governor is expecting us."

Nodding, Joseph fell in beside Lucas but remained silent. He knew that his friend was fighting a battle that was leaving a bitter taste in his mouth.

The warm greeting that the Governor extended them, as they were ushered in by an aide, let Joseph know that Lucas had not given the man any hint as to why they were there. Sitting down on small leather settee across from the Governor's desk, Lucas was the first one to speak.

"Sir, we have some questions we need to ask you, and I expect you not to be too happy about being asked."

Looking from Lucas to Joseph, the Governor frowned. His only comment was, "Alright, ask."

"McCain was murdered by poison administered by a prison guard over a period of a few days, hoping it would not bring cause for a full investigation," Joseph told the

Governor.

"Just another prisoner dying of just cause," Lucas added.

Glancing at Lucas, the Governor frowned, and asked, "Do you know which guard?"

Before Lucas could answer, Joseph said, "Yes Sir, and he's ready to talk, once we guarantee him some kind of deal."

"What kind of deal?" The Governor questioned.

Joseph's speech slowed, as he watched the fleeting expressions on the Governor's face. "Our guard tells us he was approached by a friend of yours, Governor. This man told our guard that he was there with your blessing to do whatever needed to be done to keep McCain from talking."

It was clear that the Governor was stunned, and for the moment, at a loss for words, but it did not take long for him to bounce back with red-hot anger.

"Whoever the guy is, he is a lying son-of-a-bitch. I assume you have this bastard's name?" He all but spits the words, he is so furious.

Lucas looked at Joseph, who nodded, signaling that he should tell the Governor.

"The guard says the guy claimed to be a retired General and a close friend of yours."

"Pete Mullins?" the Governors questioned.

"Yes Sir, General Mullins. That's why I wanted to see your reactions when we told you. Otherwise, we could have done it over the phone." Joseph informed him.

"I sure as hell can't blame you for that." Looking at Lucas, who was still looking extremely uncomfortable about the allegations, the Governor smiled, and said, "It's okay, Lucas, I would have handled things the same way if it had been you being cast in suspicion."

"Well sir, I have to tell you Lucas never for a moment believed it," Joseph informed the Governor, and to try to help Lucas feel a little better about himself.

"Thanks, Mate," was Lucas' acknowledgment of Joseph's jester, but follows with a question. "So, what's our first step from here."

Frowning, the Governor looked at Joseph and asked, "You think Mullins has any inkling that you have his assassin?"

"No Sir, the warden has a lid on it. He's wary and doesn't trust anyone right now," Joseph said. "You got any ideas how we should proceed? We certainly are willing to listen."

"Since it would be our assassin's word against Mullins,' we don't have a lot of evidence to go on," Joseph explained, slowly letting his brain catch up with his adrenaline. "What we need to do is get a look at Mullins computer files," he throws out to Lucas and the Governor, adding, "If either of you has a suggestion as to how we can do that, I'm willing to listen."

The three sat in silence, each contemplating the next move. It was either they were bone weary tired, or their brains had jumped a gear. The Governor was the first to break the silence.

"I am assuming that neither of you two is a computer whiz?" he inquires, with a touch of humor.

Both men shake their heads, but Joseph had another answer to offer, saying, "We may not be, but Samantha Wiggins is."

"And who might Ms. Samantha Wiggins be?" was the Governor's next question.

Joseph and Lucas answer in sync, "Sheriff Jonathan Lawrence's new bride."

Silent for a brief moment, the Governor leaned back in his chair, a crooked smile on his lips, he inquired, "And you think that the Sheriff's new bride would be willing to hack General Mullins' personal computer?"

Lucas looked at Joseph, to assure the Governor that he was not as familiar with the Sheriff or his bride.

"Samantha Lawrence was Samantha Wiggins long before she married, and she was a top-notch investigative reporter. She didn't become that without knowing how to go after information, which these times it's always on a computer."

The Governor had to agree, but he was still skeptical. "Just how do you see Mrs. Lawrence gaining access to the General's computer?

Grinning, Joseph admitted, "Now that one I haven't figured out as of yet."

'Well," the Governor said, putting heavy weight on what he asked next. "You do realize, getting evidence illegally will be of little use to us in a court of law? So, knowing and doing something with the information has a gap."

"Yeah," Joseph said, agreeing with the Governor, but

he had a "but" to add. "What we find could give us the door to go through to get the legal evidence we will need." A grin that could only be described as evil spread across Lucas' face, as he added, "Or maybe there could be just enough information leaked for our hombres across the border to come and give Mullins a ride in their chopper like they did the Senator."

Shaking his head, the Governor gave a firm "no." "I want him in court. I want him stripped of all the glory he has enjoyed, being one of our country's heroes. I want him to spend the rest of his life in a dark hole."

Smiling, Joseph nodded, saying, "Now all we have to do is figure out how to get Samantha in the General's office?"

Lucas tried to hide a grin spreading across his face, as he gave the two men his answer to Joseph's question. "Seems easy enough. Just put her in a pair of faded overalls, a bandana over her head, a cap on top, a mop bucket, a cleaning trolley, and she becomes the 'building maintenance.' Not unusual, in fact, the norm for cleaning crews to be inside offices mopping up the days grime."

Nodding, Joseph agreed that Lucas had a good idea,

but added, "I ain't so worried about her getting in as I am at getting the Sheriff to agree to let it happen."

From the stunned look on Jonathan's face, it was obvious that the idea did not appeal to him. In a slow, soft voice, he said, "Tell me, in your right mind, did you really believe I would go along with such a ludicrous idea?"

Before either man could answer, Samantha, who was seated next to Joseph, interceded, asking, "And what, pray tell, is so ludicrous about it? I have hacked computers before. I was an investigative reporter if you recall. I worked for one of the largest newspapers in this country and, I might add, I was a damn good reporter too."

And that was the end of Jonathan's objection.

CHAPTER 16

Joseph glanced at his wristwatch. It was half past midnight, and the General was just leaving to go home. Dressed in a brown jumpsuit, his long black braid tucked up under an Astro ball cap, it would have been hard for anyone to give a clear description of him, that is if anyone even looked at him. People passing seem to ignore someone pushing the cleaning trolley down the hall, and they never made eye contact with janitorial workers in the buildings.

Arriving at the office door with the sign, "Freedom First" on it, Joseph took the door key from Samantha who was standing beside him, nodded silently. She was dressed as fashionably as he was, and Joseph had to admit he thought she added class to the word janitor and their apparel. Unlocking the door, Joseph smiled, saying, "Well, entering we will now be in the criminal banks as thieves."

Giving him a stern look, Samantha retorted, "Thanks a lot."

Turning on the lights, Joseph pointed to the one and only desk in the office, and said, "There's your target."

Going over to the desk, Samantha sat down, pushed the button, and started raffling through the desk while the computer was clicking on.

Watching her, Joseph asked, "You looking for something?"

Nodding, Samantha answered, "Yes, you would be surprised how many people leave their password written down on a sticker note in their desk."

Picking up a small pad, she turned it over. Smiling, she held it up for Joseph to see. "HA! And here it is."

Two hours later, Samantha stood stretched her back, then sat back down and continued her search. Across the room, stretched out on a sofa, Joseph shook his head as he questioned, "How much more do you think is in that thing?"

Glancing at him, she smiled, "Why do you ask?"

Checking the clock on the wall above her head, he told her, "Well, seeing as it is already eleven o'clock, and I figure if you think you are going to be much longer," Joseph paused, before saying, "I can stage a break-in and we could take the computer and get the hell out of here."

Thinking about what he had said, Samantha's smile widened as she signed off on the computer and started disconnecting the computer cords. "Well, since we can't use anything I've found so far in any court, sure won't make a lot of difference if we steal the computer."

Swinging his legs off the sofa, Joseph stood up grinning as he tossed the sofa cushions onto the floor. Thirty minutes later, the office looked very much trashed and ransacked, with only the computer missing. Getting out of the building with the computer, and not running into any other cleaning staff, proved to be sticky, but the two made it out. Once they were in the car and on the way home, Samantha took a deep breath, released it slowly, and finally relaxed.

Realizing what they had just done, they looked at each other and burst out into laughter. With tears streaming down, Joseph wipes at his eyes, telling her, "Hell woman, we are going to be wanted fugitives."

Laughing, Samantha could only imagine what Jonathan would have to say. A short while later, she heard. She would have had to be deaf not to have heard.

"You did what!" Staring at Joseph and his bride, Jonathan was also trying hard not to laugh at the image the two had just painted for him. "Are you two crazy?" he asked, and followed with, "Joseph, I'm not surprised at you, but I thought better of you, Sam."

Trying to look ashamed, Samantha hung her head ever so slightly, passed a quick grin at Joseph and said, in a soft, contrite voice, "I know, we should have given it more thought, Sweetheart, but we were afraid we were going to be caught."

Joining in, Joseph added, "Yeah, we had to get out, been there way too long. We had to take the computer."

Glaring at both of them, there was no way Jonathan was buying their story, as he made the last inquiry. "I can assume you took care not to leave any fingerprints?"

"Yeah," Joseph was quick to answer. "We wiped everything down."

Giving up, Jonathan turned his question to the computer files. "Since you stole the computer, I can also assume the files are of importance?"

This time it was Samantha who answered. "It looks like the General has built himself a fair size of

Mercenaries. They called themselves Texas Liberators, and they are stationed in South Africa, Iraq, Mexico, and Iran. Supposedly, they are working with the local militia, training."

"Training them for what? Jonathan questioned.

"Supposedly, to overthrow the heads of government. That is all except the group in Mexico. From what I can determine, they plan on liberating Texas."

Joseph, who had been leaning back in his chair with his eyes closed, jerked forward. "You're kidding! Texas?" he asked, very much awake now.

Nodding, Samantha told them, "It sounds crazy, but from what I've seen so far, that is what he has in mind. The drug money, the Cartel; that's where the money to fund the General's little dream is coming from."

"How does the General plan on taking over?" Jonathan asked.

"From what I can tell, he really isn't just planning on seceding from the U S. The plans are to capture the capital, the Governor, and anyone else present at the time. He is going to force the Governor to resign and demand that the President recognize the new and independent country of

Texas. Once the Governor is out of office, those in charge will put General Mullins in as the head of the new Republic of Texas. The National Guard, the Rangers, and any other state law agencies will swear allegiance to the Republic."

Shaking his head, Lucas questioned, "Now even to these ears that sounds like seceding. How come you say that's not what he intends?"

"Mainly because of his escape plan." Seeing the questioning looks on each of their faces, Samantha explained. "The General knows the US isn't going to hand Texas over to anyone. He also knows the Governor isn't going to resign. His Mercenaries are quietly slipping out of their assigned locations in other parts of the world. They will be waiting for the General in a sweet little spot in South Africa where there is no extradition and where the General will join them."

"So, what's the point of the big grab?" was Joseph's question.

Before Samantha could answer, Jonathan spoke up. "No one is going to be watching the banks. He is planning on emptying them while the country is distracted."

Smiling at her husband's astuteness, Samantha added, "The men with him, when the Governor is grabbed, will be left behind. They are expendable. Of course, I gather from what I read they do not know that little detail."

Glancing at his wall clock, Jonathan announced, "It's three a. m., what do you say are our chances are of getting this computer back in the General's office and cleaning up whatever mess you two made and leaving things like they were?"

A crooked smile was an acknowledgment of what Jonathan was thinking. "I'd say if we hitched a ride in the chopper, put Lucas and me down on the roof, we can be in and out in less than thirty minutes."

"Why Lucas and not me? I'm the computer expert here, not Lucas," Samantha demanded to know.

Grinning, Lucas shook his head, saying, "I know enough how to connect the thing back up. Also, I figure I might be just a little bit better at breaking into a building than you."

Jonathan agreed, telling Samantha, "Just make sure the computer doesn't show any footprints. We want to catch the General in the act of treason and put him in front of a firing squad." Standing, he looked at Joseph and told him, "You know, if you two get caught, you are on your own. We can't have the Governor involved in this."

Standing, Joseph and Lucas say in unison, "Understood."

Studying each man's face, Jonathan knew that both would never lay down their guns, but would their lives, before allowing anything to touch the Governor. He wasn't sure if he was proud of the two hard-nosed idiots, or if he wanted to punch them out for being such idiots. The three of them were walking into the fire, and what was unbelievable about the whole thing was that they were doing it without a gun to their head.

Sitting the chopper down on the roof of an office building in the middle of a large city like Houston was no big thing. Helicopter landing pads on top of multi-story buildings in large commercial districts had become a common sight. Breaking into a building from the roof would hardly be noticed, but of course, that depended on if they set off any alarms.

Getting into the building from the rooftop door was relatively easy for Lucas, which made Joseph wonder just how many doors the Aussie had broken into. They were four stories above the general's office and took only moments to make their way down. Cautiously opening the door leading into the hall of the eleventh floor, Joseph peered through the slight opening. Seeing that the hallway was clear, the two walked quickly to the general's office door. Again, Lucas impressed Joseph with his ability to open locked doors, however, this time he did not let it pass, as he asked, sarcastically, "Lucas, just out of curiosity, how many break-ins have you done?"

Glancing over his shoulder as he pushes the office door open, Lucas shrugged his shoulders, saying, "Enough to know how."

Hooking the computer back up was Lucas' job, while Joseph went about straightening the office. Finally, standing back, Joseph surveyed the office. Satisfied that things were as they should be, he told Lucas, "Lets' get out of here."

CHAPTER 17

Considering that none of them had slept in the past twenty-four hours, Joseph was not surprised they all were glassy-eyed and a little looney, but plans had to be made before another day passed.

Lillian walked in with cups of fresh coffee and croissants loaded with sausage, eggs, and cheese from Sonic's to help liven them up. Samantha sat the tray down on Jonathan's desk and passed out the refreshments. Once everyone was sipping hot coffee and enjoying every morsel of the warm croissants, Jonathan started the conversation.

"Lucas, you need to go talk to the Governor. Fill him in on what we know. Not how we know; he needs to be able to claim deniability."

Nodding, Lucas kept on with his task at hand, finishing his breakfast, figuring the sheriff did not need any verbal exchange from him.

Accepting Lucas' nod, Jonathan continued, "The

Governor's birthday barbeque is being held at his ranch outside of Fredericksburg in ten days. He holds it every year on the first Saturday following the actual date. What are the chances that's when the General is going to make his move?"

Lillian, who had been sitting quietly next to Joseph, mulling over a question that had been bothering her, gave up wondering, and asked, "You guys do realize that other than Lucas, who works for the Governor, you have no jurisdiction anywhere other than in this county?"

Smiling, Jonathan nodded. "Yes ma'am, unless a felony is being committed in front of me. Which, if I understand the law, kidnapping is a felony"

With her question answered, Lillian settled back and tried not to think of the danger Joseph, Lucas, and the Sheriff were going to walk into.

"The Governor hasn't announced any plans or sent out any invitations to his barbeque, has he?" Jonathan asked, looking at Lucas.

"Not that I am aware of," Lucas said. "Usually he just calls up a few friends and invites them out. Why?"

Samantha, who was beginning to understand her newly

acquired husband's way of thinking, answered for him.

"Because he wants to make out the guest list," She told Lucas.

Jonathan acknowledged the truth of Samantha's statement by saying, "The guest list will consist of those we trust and those that are able to back us up if it comes down to a fight." Seeing Samantha and Lillian both sit forward, ready to do battle themselves, Jonathan quickly added, "I do not think it will come down to any firefight. The men the General brings with him might be willing to, but I do not think the General is totally willing to take a bullet for a few dollars."

Grinning, Lucas told him, "Well, Mate, I ain't sure when a few million dollars became a few dollars to you, but you might just have the General figured wrong."

"You could be right," Jonathan acknowledged. "The guest list is going to be stacked, just in case. We take him and his men when they are off guard when they would lest expect any trouble."

Standing, Lucas told him, "While you and Joseph lay the groundwork, I will make the Governor aware of the latest."

Jonathan nodded in agreement. "You might grab a few hours of sleep before heading back to Austin."

Grinning, Lucas agreed. "Plan on doing just that." Giving the room a half salute, Lucas left to call the Governor.

Joseph, who had not said much up to this point, questioned, "Just who you plan on putting on this guest list."

"Company F of the Texas Rangers out of Waco, you, Lucas, me and a couple of friends that were Special Forces."

Nodding, Joseph asked, "Why not the National Guard? Think the General might have corrupted them?"

"No!" Jonathan was quick to banish that thought. He went on to explain, "Calling out the National Guard would set off a lot of questions. About ten of the Rangers, we three, and a couple of friends, if we handle things right, should be enough."

"You don't figure we will be outnumbered if there is a fight?" Joseph questioned.

"No, because as far as the General will know, there is only going to be four other guests. The bar-be-que will be held when its dark outside, where floodlights will be needed for incoming. It's being held as a campaign strategy meeting for the Governor's re-election," Jonathan explained.

"Why night; why floodlights?" was Joseph's quick inquiry.

"I figure the General and a driver will be coming by car. His little army will come by chopper. Quick in, and quick out."

"And, what better way to blind than with floodlights," Joseph says, with an understanding nod.

Before Joseph could comment, Samantha spoke up. "And, as a reporter, I will be there to get pictures and statements out to the voters."

Both Jonathan and Joseph opened their mouth to say a resounding, "no," but before one sound can be uttered, Lillian jumped in, "And I am there representing the Black Caucus voters."

Not ready to give the men a chance for argument, Samantha inquired, "If the man is giving a bar-be-que at his home, don't you think there would be a woman or two for his wife to talk with?"

Now, that was an argument that Jonathan had an answer for. "The Governor's wife won't be there. She's visiting her mother, who lives in Denver."

"Doesn't matter; Governor isn't going to get re-elected without the black vote," was Lillian's rebuttal.

"And without the press giving him lots of coverage, he is dead in the waters," Samantha added. "So, don't you think the General would at least expect someone there, from the black voters and the press?"

Knowing they had lost the argument, Jonathan agreed. "When I tell you to leave, you both make a beeline for the farthest root cellar, understood?"

Both women nod in agreement. They were not going to push the requirement for their stay that would come later. But, Samantha had one last question.

"Just what part are you going to play in this little one-act play?"

"Well, seeing as a couple of my fellow military friends are willing to be the first on the ground, I plan on being with them."

Joseph spoke up before Samantha could object to Jonathan's plan. "I figure I will be with you. We need to coordinate the whole thing, and Lucas isn't going to like being left out."

"I know," Jonathan said, and added, "but I want him with the Governor. If there is any unexpected trouble, it will be up to him to take the General out."

Samantha knew there were no guarantees to a long life, but she certainly did not like listening to Jonathan casually telling how he was about to put his life in the line of fire. She was sure Lillian was not feeling any differently where Joseph was concerned. Samantha also realized that being a small-town sheriff had its dangers, but this was not a small-town action, and not one she was prepared for.

Back at home, and the two of them alone, she let Jonathan know how she was feeling, by demanding, "If these men who you are willing to walk into fire with know their job, why do you have to be with them?"

Jonathan opened the refrigerator door, removed two beers, opened them and handed one to Samantha. He then led the way into the den where he crashed on the sofa. Leaning his head back, he spoke in comforting tones, explaining the "why" to his new bride.

"The men we are talking about would walk into fire if

I asked them to. They did it more than once. I cannot, nor will not ask them to do something I would not do."

Samantha remained silent for several minutes, studying her husband. Finally, taking a deep breath, she released it slowly. She sat down next to him on the sofa and leaned over and place her head on his shoulder, telling him, "I love you, and I know you will do what you believe is right. Just try not to get yourself killed. I'm too young to be a widow so soon."

Taking hold of her hand, Jonathan stood, pulling her up with him and in a swift movement and swung her up into his arms. Kissing the top of her head, he told her, "We need sleep. Tomorrow we will find ways to enjoy our few remaining honeymoon days."

Nestling her face into his neck, Samantha managed a sigh and a soft "Hmm."

Lillian had waited until she and Joseph were back at her house before she voiced her thought s about the General and the plans to take him down. Entering the house, she turned took Joseph's hand, and continuing to her bedroom, she informed him, "If you are going to insist on trying to get yourself killed, you are going to make me a papoose, so I will have someone to love."

Not having any ready argument on the tip of his tongue, Joseph kept quiet and followed Lillian meekly into the bedroom.

CHAPTER 18

Standing a few feet away from the company of men Jonathan had called upon, Joseph could tell they all were experienced in combat. Their moods were light, showing no stress at all. It was like they were out for a fun night of camping and comradeship of old friends. Glancing down at Sam, who was sitting quietly beside him, he spoke softly. "Sam, old girl, I think we are in a company of warriors." As though she understood exactly what he said, Sam pressed against his leg in agreement.

Jonathan's walkie-talkie interrupted Joseph's train of thought, as the posted gate guard announced, "A blue, four-door Ford, two female passengers, followed by a black sedan, two male passengers."

The casual lightheartedness that the small group of men had been exhibiting vanished immediately and the warriors that Joseph had called them were standing ready.

From his vantage point, Joseph watched as the two

automobiles pulled up in front of the low rambling ranch house. General Mullins and his driver got out and walked over to Samantha and Lillian. The four walked toward the front entrance talking in what seemed like, to the observer, a friendly conversation. Perfectly innocent, but if so, why the creeping spider crawling up his spin? Before any action could be taken on his part, the scrambled voice on the walkie-talkie came back with, "Incoming chopper, estimate two clicks out."

Whatever action Joseph might have given thought to was vanquished as the overhead lights in the barn were shut off and the interior of the barn was clothed in darkness. With the lights extinguished, night vision goggles were quickly put on. They did not have to wait long before the whirling sounds of the helicopter blades were heard. Jonathan slowly slid the side door of the barn open to have visual sight of the approaching chopper.

Watching the helicopter come in low, just above the treetops, Joseph was surprised at how silent the whirling blades seem to be. It was doubtful that the sound could be heard inside the house. The slow setting down of the chopper did not even seem to bother the blades of glass it came to rest on. Once the chopper touched grown, the door slid back, and six heavily armed men jumped out. Their boots hitting the ground triggered the floodlights to come on, flooding the area with light brighter than the sun. "Lay down your arms!" was blasted over the temporary loudspeaker systems that Jonathan had installed.

If it was expected that the men would lay down their guns and surrender, it came as a surprise that the opposite happened. One dropped to his knee, firing toward the floodlights, while the other five broke for the house. Joseph, Jonathan, and the remaining men charged the barn door, firing at the fleeing men.

Inside the house, Lucas, who was in the kitchen filling a pitcher full of lemonade, heard the first shot. Dropping the pitcher, Lucas darted for the door, pulling his gun as he ran.

On the enclosed terrace, the Governor, General Mullins, and the General's assistant, Russell Winslow, all heard the gunfire at the same time. Winslow pulled his gun, stepped up beside Lillian, and softly told her, "Stay calm, and no one will get hurt." These words were spoken just as Lucas came through the door.

"Drop your gun, Lucas," Mullins ordered, adding, "no one need get hurt." He grabbed Samantha's arm and pulled her against him as he pressed his gun against her rib cage.

Lucas' brain registered the fact that Mullins' driver was gripping Lillian's arm with his gun pressed to her side. Mullins had his left arm around Samantha's waist with his gun jammed into her ribs.

"HOLD," Lucas said, his voice rising just a little more than he intended. "You don't have a chance, General. We can all walk away from this; just put down your guns."

"Can't do that, my boy. Never surrender, is our motto." Mullins said as he moved Samantha closer to the outside door.

"Lucas is right, General," Samantha said, with a slight shake in her voice. "Your men have been arrested or killed by now. There is no money being transferred to your offshore account."

Lucas joined in informing Mullins of what was happening or had already happened. "Your guy that you set up to hack into the Banks is either dead or in cuffs. You won't walk away from this, unscratched, but you can stay alive."

Shaking his head, Mullins snorted a half laugh, saying, "And spend the rest of my life in some cell? No thanks. Now I am going to walk out of here, get in that chopper outside, and when me and my men are safe, I'll send the women back."

Jabbing the gun barrel into Samantha's, side he snarled, "Now drop your gun or I'll put a bullet in the lady," he ordered.

Holding his left arm up, palm forward, Lucas lowered his gun in his right hand, slightly. Keeping his voice steady, Lucas moved ever so slightly to his left, and in his peripheral vision, saw Mullins' henchman shift his gun from Lillian's rib cage to cover him.

"The law dogs will STRIKE you….," emphasis was placed on the word, "strike," and with the utterance, a flash of grey passes in front of him, as Sam charged Mullins on his blind side. Concurrently, two shots rang out, and Mullins' man falls, with two bullets piercing his chest. Simultaneously, Sam hit Mullins in the chest, knocking him down. As he falls, his gun discharges, shattering the overhead light, and in concert, his ear-piercing scream could be heard as Sam's fangs clamp down into his gun arm.

Within the same breath, Joseph and Jonathan charge through the outside door as Lucas gave the command, "Off," to Sam. He then bends down and picks up Mullins' gun, warning, "Make one move and I'll let her finish you off." Darting a frightening look toward Sam, who was sitting quietly less than a couple of feet away, Mullins nodded his understanding.

As Joseph gathers Lillian in his arms, she managed a shaky smile, and asked, "What took you so long?"

A short laugh escaped Lucas, releasing his taut nerves. "Yeah, Mate, what took you so long?" he inquired.

Jonathan, who had his arm around Samantha, pointed at Sam. Smiling, he told him, "I'd say you got that dog pretty well trained. She was just the diversion you and Joseph needed to take out Mullins' henchman. You might want to reconsider letting her go to Joseph, seeing how well the two of you work together."

"Yes, sir. Was going to talk to Joseph about that very thing," Lucas said. Looking at Joseph, he apologetically adds, "Sorry, Mate, you're not going to have much time for Sam, with a new bride and all. Besides, you need to train your own sidekick."

Knowing Lucas was right, Joseph nodded, saying, "I expect you to find that pup, be my wedding present from you."

A big smile spread across Lucas' face, as he nodded. "That I will do. Now let's get this bunch of traitors loaded up and go have a wedding."

The wedding ceremony itself was small and intimate, with only Samantha, Jonathan, Joseph, Lillian, and Lucas present. The wedding vows were officiated by the local justice to assure Lillian that all was right in her beliefs. Blessings were said by the pastor of the small Baptist church she attended. And to appease Joseph's ancestors, the ancient Native American ceremonies were performed.

Standing on the banks of the Trinity, the bride was dressed in a long, white dress made of deerskin, with fringe on the sleeves and colorful beads circling the neck and hem. Her knee-high boots were made of white deerskin. As she stood beside Jonathan, who was standing in for her father, they awaited the groom. From the edge of the forest, Joseph emerged, leading a beautiful midnight black Mustang with a reef of wildflowers around its neck.

Walking up to stand in front of Jonathan, he handed the lead rope on the horse to Jonathan who took it and stepped back, offering Lillian's hand to Joseph. Taking her hand, Joseph led Lillian to the flower-layered canoe that awaited them. As Lillian stepped into the canoe, a loud, eagle's screech was heard above them. Joseph looked up and smiled, and in his native tongue, spoke, "Hello, Grandfather. I am happy you could make my blessed day."

With another loud screech, the magnificent eagle soared into the clouds, and out of sight.

THE END

MEET THE AUTHOR

Sue Land

Sue Land is native Texan and is devoted to preserving Texas culture and history. She is an active historian and has written and been involved in filmmaking for more than twenty-five years. In addition to being the author of the *Digger* mystery book series, Sue is the Director and Producer for Swanee Productions, an independent film company, as well as the Director and Publicist for the Billy the Kid Museum in Hico, Texas.

Made in the USA
Las Vegas, NV
22 March 2023